Metaphorosis

June 2019

Beautifully made speculative fiction

Also from Metaphorosis Books

Score – an SFF symphony

Reading 5X5: Readers' Edition
Reading 5X5: Writers' Edition

Best Vegan Science Fiction & Fantasy

Best Vegan SFF of 2018
Best Vegan SFF of 2017
Best Vegan SFF of 2016

Metaphorosis Magazine

Metaphorosis: Best of 2018
Metaphorosis: Best of 2017
Metaphorosis: Best of 2016

Metaphorosis 2018: The Complete Stories
Metaphorosis 2017: The Complete Stories
Metaphorosis 2016: Nearly Complete Stories

Monthly issues

by B. Morris Allen

Susurrus
Allenthology: Volume I
Tocsin: and other stories
Start with Stones: collected stories
Metaphorosis: a collection of stories

Metaphorosis

June 2019

edited by
B. Morris Allen

Metaphorosis Books

Neskowin

ISSN: 2573-136X (online)
ISBN: 978-1-64076-141-4 (e-book)
ISBN: 978-1-64076-142-1 (paperback)

June 2019

Country Whispers.....................................7
by Matthew Amundsen

The Thousand Revolutions of Kronstadt..43
by Pablo Valcarcel

Las Vegas Museum of Space Exploration 83
by Marilee Dahlman

The Girls Who Come Back Are Made of
Metal and Glass.....................................99
by L'Erin Ogle

Country Whispers

Matthew Amundsen

Seeing the bodies of them girls hanging outside the town's gates made me think coming here was a bad idea, but it was too late to go back now. The driver, Finnas, didn't seem the type to turn these horses around no matter what I said, and Maw would send me right back even if he did. The kitties dangling alongside the girls made me feel worse. I didn't know if the girls did anything bad to anybody, but I knew for sure those kitties never hurt anyone. Witches, that told me, but who knew if it was true. Town folk tend to blame natural things they don't understand on witches.

Finnas shoved my head back between the haystacks and told me to keep my mouth shut. Just as well. I didn't want to see any more.

Snapping the reins, he drove the cart through the gates. Since it was almost nighttime, the town was quiet. All I heard was the rumble of the wheels until we came to a stop. He hopped down quick, and I heard him heave and grunt as some big doors groaned open. He jumped back up and drove the cart a little ways more before stopping for good. Somebody said something and he got down again.

I stuck out my head and saw a tall, fancy-dressed lady standing in a dusty courtyard surrounded by a fence taller than two men. Just beyond was a wide house, bigger than any I'd ever seen. Finnas tried to give her a hug and a kiss, but she pushed him off and cocked her head at me. I sucked in air and ducked down, but it was too late. The woman had spotted me.

"You girl, come down here."

My face burning like a kid caught stealing a pie, I climbed down from the cart to show myself.

"Are you Leusa Wrothburn?"

"Yes'm." I ducked my head down like Maw said I should, but I couldn't bring myself to curtsy. Just ain't something I'm much good at. I didn't see what the big deal was anyway. This woman had no reason to make me feel bad for being who I was. From the look of her, she was a tough bird, but I hadn't done anything to be ashamed of.

"Do you know where you are?"

"Yes'm. I reckon we're in the town of Stonefeld."

"Correct. And do you know who I am?"

I gave her another look without trying to be nosy. "No, ma'am, but I reckon you're somebody important by your fancy dress and the size of this here house."

"Good. Maybe you're not as simple as they said you were. I'm Ulna Fustable. The Magistrate of Stonefeld is my husband. I don't know if you've heard way out in the woods where your folk are from, but he's been having some problems with witches." She said the word like it was something too nasty to say out loud but she had to anyway. All I could think about when she said it was those poor kitties strung up with the girls at the town's gate. "We need another serving girl around here after the last one was found to be lacking, and my husband doesn't trust any of the girls from town. The birth register said you have a sister. That true?"

"Yes'm. Tessa's working for a family over in Brasston now." Daft cow got herself seeded by one of the lord's manservants, but the Magistrate's wife didn't need to know that.

"Your mama all alone now?"

I nodded. This lady was sharp.

"I'll make sure she gets your pay then. Nothing you can spend it on around here anyway."

I wanted to say that Maw didn't deserve anything from me on account of the way she treats me, but just this once I kept my mouth shut. I wasn't happy about it but complaining never solved anything.

"You'll do anything you're asked— laundry, sweep, help prepare food. I expect you to be the first one up in the morning and the last one to sleep. Don't talk to any of the other serving girls unless spoken to, and stay out of my husband's way. Understand that you are not allowed beyond these walls. The last thing my husband needs is gossiping townsfolk." She looked me up and down to make sure I'd been listening. "All that sit okay with you?"

"Yes'm."

"Good. You can stay in the room next to the stable for now. Supper's in the kitchen but it's cold. Finnas will show you."

"Thank you, ma'am," I said. Seemed the right thing to say.

"And get that straw out of your hair, girl. Try to look proper."

Finnas unhitched the horses from the cart, and I followed him.

"Over there," he said, pointing at a door.

"Aye."

The room was nothing but a closet under the stairs that led to Finnas' loft. Maw told me I had to sleep inside if the Fustables told me to. Town folk look down on them who sleep outside, like we were some kind of animal. Maybe I was an animal. Didn't bother me none. Animals never did wrong to nobody who didn't deserve it.

Through the wall, I heard them horses hassling Finnas because he didn't understand them. He thought sugar cubes and a switch was the answer to everything. When they finally gave up and quieted, he trudged up the stairs to his room. His boots boomed when they hit the floor. He never did show me where they kept the leftovers. Didn't matter. I wasn't hungry.

I tried to sleep, but couldn't. Rooms and I never got along, and this one felt like as much of a jail as any other. The stillness and the quiet suffocated me. At least I could smell the horses through the walls. That was some comfort, anyway.

In the middle of the night, a door from the house sighed open, feet scuffed the courtyard and then someone stalked the stairs above my room. Finnas' bed creaked for a while overhead, and then that someone came back down. Wasn't my business who, though I had a guess.

I waited another hour or two before getting up to take a look around the courtyard and see what I could do to stay busy. First thing I noticed was a measly stack of logs next to the kitchen. Place this size always needs firewood. Problem was, I didn't see an ax anywhere and I wasn't about to go rattling the stable doors and get Finnas after me at this hour.

Since no one else was around, I wandered around the back of the stables, out of sight of the main house. The property went only a little farther before the fence hemmed it in. Clusters of hospras grew here, stiff and unhappy. I felt bad for them trees, trapped here while others grew free on the other side of the fence, where there weren't no folks to tame them into lesser versions of themselves.

I dropped a seed and sprouted a taccab leaf from it with a few quiet words. I dried it with a hush and rolled it into a smoke, which helped me think about what to do with what I been dealt. Something itched my scalp as I stood there sucking that taccab, telling me I found what I forgot I was looking for. I pinched the cherry off the taccab and kicked around in the scrub until I felt that unsettled thing. There.

Trapped under a bush thick with long grass and vines, a dull throbbing ax head stuck atop a shriveled handle. Rusted and forgotten, I knew how to make it feel better. Metal was dangerous to whisper, but I could see this poor tool needed my help. I reminded the blade of when it was properly seasoned and sharp and full o' glory, and it responded in kind. I told the shrunken handle how it used to be stout and firm, fit to be swinging. At first ashamed at its fallen state, it soon remembered its bold peak and found its shape again. Now I could do my job.

A bunch of the hospras weren't tended proper, and leaned over as if all their life had dripped out already. I listened for the right ones calling for mercy. Taking care since people was sleeping, I asked the sound to turn inside-out so no one would hear. Half a dozen hospras came down that way. I chopped and split and stacked them next to the logs outside the kitchen and then continued the pile around the corner when I ran out of room. That should last them a few weeks or a month if they were frugal. The tightness in Miss Ulna's mouth made me think squandering resources was not something she tolerated.

I didn't know where the ax should rightly go, so I stuck it back under the same bush and thanked it for letting me borrow it. I asked the bush to hold the ax in its branches tight like a babe, to blanket it with leaves. Any stranger who stumbled upon it would have a hard time convincing the bush to let go.

Figuring I'd done enough for now, I climbed a thick hospra to watch the sun rise. I must have fallen asleep because the next thing I knew, the cock jumped up and told everybody what was on his mind.

I heard scuffling from the kitchen and jumped down to wait outside the door. With a mop of grey curls and a long-faded apron, the cook looked like she'd been sampling her own creations for years. Which was a good sign, since nobody trusted skinny cooks anyway. Yawning, she grabbed a couple of logs for morningfire, saw the new stacks I'd made and stood in shock. She jumped like she saw a ghost when she noticed me hovering.

"You must be the new girl. Miss Ulna told me to look out for you." She followed the stack of wood around the corner. "You see who did this?"

"I chopped the wood, ma'am."

She looked me up and down, suspicious. "You? In one night? In the dark?"

"Yes, ma'am. The moon was plenty bright."

She narrowed her eyes like she didn't believe me. "How come nobody woke up?"

Maw told me not to do my whispers in town 'cause people will think I'm a witch or such. I been called worse by Maw herself in one of her moods, but I seen how this town treated girls they didn't like, and their cats, so I figured Maw's advice made as much sense as any.

I shrugged. "I did it quiet."

She looked at me like I was trying to be smart with her, but I didn't smile or nothing and she let it go. Looking again at the woodpile, she stepped close to me, wide-eyed and whispering so no one would overhear. "Did you use an ax?"

I chuckled at this. "How else do you chop wood?"

Her voice grew stern. "This ain't a laughing matter, country girl. Didn't you see what the menfolk did to those poor girls when you came here?"

I started to worry a little. "Hard to miss."

"No woman in town is allowed to use a metal blade or anything with a sharp edge."

Stonefeld was even worse than I imagined. "That's crazy talk."

The cook huffed. "You don't know the half of it. But things are gonna change real soon."

Didn't seem likely, but no point arguing.

She took another look at me and must have noticed the simple way I dressed in clothes I'd sown myself, with hair I cut without so much as looking in a river for a reflection. "I don't suppose you get much news about Stonefeld where you're from."

"Nothing that happened in this town was any of my business before today."

"Well, you best make it your business now. Yet I can't lie, we needed that wood. So, thanks for that. Play dumb around Finnas and Miss Ulna if they ask you about it. I get the feeling you're smarter than they think."

"I don't know about that, ma'am." I smiled despite myself.

"Save that 'ma'am' business for Miss Ulna. Call me Makzeet."

She stuck out her hand, and I gave it the customary one-shake like men do. "Leusa."

"Don't wander too far in case I need you later, but steer clear of the menfolk. They're no good. Us women got to stick together."

I found a broom and swept up the courtyard some until Makzeet had me fetch eggs from the coop. I felt a little bad telling them hens I was gonna treat their eggs nice, but they had to believe that so they wouldn't peck me when I swiped their unborn babies. The eggs were pretty blues and browns, sometimes a swirl of both, and I gathered them in the dopey apron Maw insisted I wear when Finnas drove me off from her place. Funny that the thing was useful after all.

I brought my bounty into the kitchen and felt someone's eyes sticking to me. I didn't dare peek who until Makzeet took the last egg from the bundle and shooed me back outside. When I ducked out the door, I looked back and saw a serving girl around my age, wearing clothes no better than mine. Her eyes said she didn't know what kind of creature I was; not scared or disgusted, only curious.

After lunch, I spied the Magistrate for the first time when Finnas helped him lurch into the wagon. Bloated and crabby, fella like that gave me the shivers just thinking about him. He and Finnas left the compound in a cloud of dust, flapping like a couple of pompous geese kicked out of a pond. I almost felt bad for the horses pulling them, though really they were happy just to get out of the stables. Being stuck in small places ain't good for nobody.

The whole place grew real quiet once their cart rumbled away. Even Makzeet knocked off somewhere, her big copper pot drying outside. Nobody was coming or going or asking for me, so I slipped around the back of the stables and found me a wide hospra I could lean against and watch the sky over the fence, dreaming of the forest where I wished I was.

Bored and homesick, I dropped another taccab seed and encouraged a tendril from it, one I sweet-talked into sprouting and bursting enough for me to pull off a few leaves. With a word, they shriveled in my hand and rolled themselves tight. I dared one to ignite and spent its length basking in the smoke of home. The home I made, not the one I came from. A couple of footsteps behind me made me pinch the roll dead, tuck it and the fresh ones under my skirt.

"Don't stop on my account." The serving girl from before sat across from me, both of us hidden from anyone who might be looking our way from the back of the house. "I was hoping you'd share."

I smiled at that and handed her a fresh one while plucking out my leftover for myself. She looked around then back at me, wondering how to light it. I'd forgotten town folk don't know the name of the flame or the proper way to talk to it.

"Is that the best you can do?" I asked. Nothing motivates fire like antagonism.

The serving girl looked at me funny, thinking I was talking to her and almost scared about it, until her roll started smoldering on its own.

"Oh," she said, nodding like she understood all along. She took a greedy drag and yakked like a badger. She smiled once she caught her breath and shook her head. "Been so long, I forgot how it was. I'm Trixa."

"Leusa."

"Nice to meet you."

She took a more practiced drag this time and grimaced only a little. "I don't know what it's like where you're from, but women are forbidden to smoke in Stonefeld."

"Between all the things women ain't supposed to do and those hangings, I got to wonder why any women live here at all."

Trixa scrunched her eyes and looked upset. Maybe I shouldn't have said anything. "Where are we supposed to go?"

She had a point. Not everyone is cut out to live by themselves in the woods like me or Maw. Just ask my sister. And even Maw insisted on a proper home with four walls and a roof. I was different than most, I guess.

"What did those dead girls do?"

Trixa scowled at me until she realized I really didn't know. Looking over my shoulder back toward the house, she whispered that the girls were found together in the woods, naked, their cats nearby. She leaned back, drifting away like the smoke from her dwindling roll.

I rolled my eyes. If these people could only see me on a warm day with nobody but the bugs, birds, and beasts watching me, they'd think me just as wicked. I couldn't say that to Trixa, though.

"Before they were hung, they said Miss Sangela put them up to it."

"Who's that?"

Trixa's jaw dropped though her smile was genuine. "You really are from the middle of nowhere, aren't you?"

I never told her that, but it was true. I'd still be there but for having to do my daughterly duty so as not to dishonor our family name or our progeny. Maw and I both knew I'd never have progeny, so I figured she meant my sister's bastard.

"Miss Sangela was our schoolteacher, but now she's going to be tried as a witch day after tomorrow. We won't let the same thing happen to her."

In a place where a girl couldn't smoke or hold a knife and had to wear clothes like a dress-up dolly, a place where being natural got you killed, I didn't see any way out of it. People who would hang cats would hang anybody for anything. No point saying that to Trixa, though. Let her have hope, if only for another day.

A door slapped against a frame, and we both jumped to our feet.

"Stay away from the Magistrate and Finnas," Trixa whispered. She ran to the kitchen before Makzeet could call her name.

I hung back, because I didn't like the way the wind stirred in the courtyard. Not much later, Finnas ran his horses through the gate, trotting them to a halt outside the Magistrate's residence. Part of me wanted to disappear among the hospras, but curiosity got the better of me. I wanted another look at the man who ran a town like this.

Heaving, corpulent, the Magistrate needed Finnas to help him down from the carriage. To his credit, Finnas spared his boss the curses he used to guide his stable. The Magistrate waddled toward his home without looking backward until he stiffened like a hound catching the stink of a fox. Me, had to be. But Finnas led him on inside, and the Magistrate never saw me. Next time I had to stay out of sight.

That night, Makzeet let me finish what was left in the pot after everyone had their fill. I didn't mind going last. The bits at the bottom had the most taste anyhow, soaking in all them flavors all day long. I even used a spoon, which woulda made Maw proud. Felt good not to have to make my own fire, cook my own food. Had to admit it tasted better than mine too.

I washed the dish I messed and went to my room. Any fresh bed I could make myself in the forest would be softer and cleaner than the lifeless flop they gave me here. I made do, though, as Maw said I had to, and fell asleep after wondering how that would ever happen in this dank box. I don't think I'd been sleeping long when the soft thump of bare feet padding up the stairs over my head woke me. The door to Finnas' quarters creaked in the stillness, and pretty soon the sound of two people trying to be quiet kept me from falling back asleep. I used their escalating rutting to hide the creak of my own door, and slipped out back. I lay tucked away between a pair of bushes I softened with flattery and flowers, and dozed off before I knew it.

Something soft and ticklish ran under my nose, waking me while the swollen moon reigned over everything. I started awake, suddenly alert, and saw a cat. The creature came back for another pass, and I reached out a hand, welcoming, accepting. I knew she was a she as soon as I touched her. She leaned into my touch, receptive, and we were friends. She swiped past me one more time and then sauntered away. Curious, I watched her go. She sensed I wasn't following her and swiveled her head over her shoulder, looking for my eyes. Smirking at the boldness of this creature I stood up and shadowed her.

This cat didn't know any better and headed for the house, which made me nervous. I knew cats were mysterious to the point of sacred, but I was pretty sure these town folk didn't feel the same way. The closer she got to the building, the faster I chased after her, until it became some kind of game. She stopped at the kitchen door and skirted aside when I caught up to her. Rubbing up against my leg and looking up at me, her mouth stretched as if mewing, but made no sound. I didn't know what she wanted until she clawed the bottom of the door and attempted to pull it open. By the marks on the wood, this wasn't the first time. This cat obviously lived here, and I was the only one who didn't know it. Should have expected the Magistrate to be a hypocrite.

"Here, girl," I said, guiding a stick through a gap in the door to unlatch it and holding the door open long enough for her to disappear inside. I couldn't latch it back, but didn't expect anyone would know the difference. Too tired to go back where I'd been, I gave my room another try. That might have been the thing that spared my life.

Some time later, I heard a muffled scream from within the house. Someone wailed at some offence, and everything stilled that heard it. Even Finnas startled in his bed above me, his snorts stifled unexpectedly aware, waiting for another shout from the dark. An erratic wail keened from the house in stops and stutters until concerned murmuring blanketed it into silence. Whatever happened in there, best I didn't know.

After that, it was quiet so long that I figured the worst was over. Even Finnas fell back asleep, by the sawing breath above me.

Yells from the house cut that short. The Magistrate opened a second floor window and shouted for us to present ourselves in the courtyard immediately. He sniffed and slammed the window shut.

Finnas came down the steps faster than I could get out of the closet underneath. Makzeet, Trixa, and half a dozen other servants filed from the house, everybody but me in their sleeping clothes. Groggy, disheveled, and confused, we lined up as asked. I looked toward the two I knew, but couldn't read their faces. We waited, nervous, but nothing happened for a long time. I wanted to go back to bed, even the pathetic one that was mine, rather than stand here.

The Magistrate finally hobbled into the courtyard to confront us. With his wife at his side, he resumed yelling for us to present ourselves as if we were the tardy ones and not his sorry self. He stabbed the air with his cane as he accosted us with a bizarre tantrum about his importance to Stonefeld and the sanctity of his lineage. He referred a couple of times to scratches and stitches and the demonic nature of felines, and I slowly pieced together what made him rave. That cat had gouged him deep and true, and he knew someone had let it in.

"That sort of vermin isn't allowed in town, let alone these premises! Do any of you understand how serious this is? I could have you all flogged—or worse!"

None of us looked him in the eye. Whenever I tried to sneak a peek, Miss Ulna stared me down. She knew. Maybe she didn't know exactly what she knew, but she knew it had something to do with me. I knew all along it wasn't right for me to live in town. I tried telling Maw and Finnas too, but no one listened, and here I was stuck where I didn't belong.

"Maybe one of you is a witch," the Magistrate spewed at last, as if confirming to himself aloud his gut instinct.

Miss Ulna reacted sharp and cross to that. "You think I'd let a witch slip past me, Harmon? I'm the one who runs this place while you're besotting yourself at the public house."

The Magistrate glowered but had no answer, looking embarrassed. His grip on his cane wobbled like he wasn't sure what to do next. He looked me up and down, seeing me for the first time. "What about that one?"

"She's nothing but a shivering little field mouse. Look at her."

I didn't agree, but played along. What her game was, I didn't know. But it worked.

"If it happens again, I'll blame you," her husband finally gruffed at her, limping away without looking back.

Miss Ulna spared us the dramatics, but not the sparks. She seethed like she was about to jump right out of her skull. "I expect you all know that felines are not welcome here. Any exceptions to this will be dealt with next time by the town council, and they will not be so forgiving as me. Is that understood?"

We said yes, almost under our breaths, but audible enough to qualify as a response.

"Good. Now leave my sight."

The moon fell before I ventured outside of my closet again. I wanted a taccab roll real bad, but couldn't risk Miss Ulna's anger if she caught a whiff. With the fear of witches in the air, now wasn't the time to take chances on little things. After last night's fiasco, I could tell the Magistrate was the type of man who looked for excuses to make people feel lesser than him. But damnation did I want a smoke.

I hid among the hospras when I heard Finnas come down for morning meal. The Magistrate's bellowing chased him from the kitchen before long. Finnas scrambled into the stables and returned with the horses and carriage. After grunts, groaning, and complaints from both him and the horses, he helped the Magistrate clamber aboard. Only when I heard the clopping hooves and strike of reins fading away did I dare venture out. Shy, I peered into the kitchen without a word until Makzeet noticed me poking around. She wiped her hands on her apron, looked over her shoulder, and waved me in.

"Quick, eat before she comes down."

Makzeet pushed a bowl of grain meal at me before I could object and sat across from me, watching me pitch it in. The look in her eye worried me some, and I swallowed without hardly chewing.

"She's in a fit this morning. You'd best make yourself scarce."

I nodded, gulping down my last mouthful. I stood and went toward the wash bucket, but Makzeet took the bowl from me and shooed me out the door.

Apologizing to a hospra for my rudeness, I climbed its low branches and asked nicely if it would turn its coarse bark smooth for a little while. Now soft, its branches snugged together to cradle me like a babe. In return, I promised it would grow tall and strong and with a few words made it safe from blade and fire. Anything less would be rude.

I was almost asleep when the back door clapped shut with a bang. From my perch, I saw Trixa carrying a basket of laundry piled as high as her head. I climbed down to help. Trixa acted like she didn't want to see me. She changed direction when she saw me coming and tried to again when I grabbed the basket. She wouldn't look me in the eyes, and I didn't know why until I remembered about the cat. Why anyone hated cats still made no sense to me, but I guess I did get everybody yelled at.

"He could have hung us all because of you," she growled at last.

"Let me help," I said. "I can do that much."

Trixa acted like she hadn't heard, but she couldn't get away if I didn't let go. She looked over her shoulder to make sure no one watched us before dropping the basket. She said nothing more while we hung the clothes and linens to dry. After a while I got tired of her silence and tried acting silly to make her laugh so she'd remember we were friends, but she didn't budge. After we hung the last sheets, I noticed we had corridors of cloth hiding us from the house. I spun around to spark a roll and turned back to Trixa with it lit only to find Miss Ulna instead. Her anger still boiled with a fury that could end me right quick.

"Did you scratch my husband?" The sheets whipped behind her like a curse.

I yelped and dropped the roll. "I never hurt nothing or nobody."

By the cooling of her face, she believed me. She nodded as if knowing my mind, acknowledging the truth of it. "You're not a shapeshifter, are you? You prefer the company of animals to people, but most of your powers lie with plants. The chopped wood, the extra flowers, the taccab. I get it." She waved her hand as if it were beneath her.

I shook my head, denying everything.

"Really, Leusa Wrothburn. Do you really think I would have hired you without knowing who you were and what you could do? That would have been irresponsible."

"How did—?"

"None of your business. But you don't have to worry about me. What you do isn't like that witch stuff. Your talent is natural."

The sheets stopped flapping behind her, my heart slowed to normal, and I calmed my breathing.

"Those girls hanging—"

"Those girls hanging are lucky. The forces they were fooling with were about to tear them apart. They are none of your concern."

The kitties were what really concerned me, but she didn't need to know that.

Miss Ulna bent toward me to speak quietly even though the drying laundry sheltered us plenty. "Trixa told you there's a trial tomorrow. Between you and me, my husband fears for his life, and wants every man in town to carry a freshly sharpened blade to the trial. Problem is, the smith can't handle it all by himself and could use some help. What do you think?"

I shook my head. "I've never done anything like that."

"That ax doesn't count?"

"It's not the same. I can't do something that might hurt somebody."

Miss Ulna leaned closer and whispered mean. "How do you think my husband will react when I tell him you were the one who put that cat in our house? Does he seem like a forgiving man to you?"

Thinking of Maw, I bowed my head. She probably wouldn't approve even if she knew I had no choice. "I don't know if I can do it, but I'll try."

Miss Ulna picked up the empty laundry basket and straightened. "Wonderful. Finnas will bring the blades to your room. Finish what you can, and he'll get them in the morning. Don't speak of this to anyone."

She left without looking back, and I climbed a tree.

Sure enough, later that afternoon, Finnas clattered into the courtyard with a loaded wagon. I didn't have to guess where he was gonna drop his cargo. No point in watching. I didn't have time to get down before he rode off and returned with another load. I wondered if there'd be a third one, but heard him putting the horses to bed. Not until he clomped up the stairs after dinner did I dare peek inside what they called my room.

I caught them preening when I walked in, their squeaks like hungry chicks. They rattled in their boxes, following me with their glittery crescent smiles topped with motley handles of different makes, different ages, and different life experiences. Maw always said never to walk with metal, said it so much I couldn't tell if it was her powers of insistence or a motherly warning. But I saw them now and understood how easy it was to fall in love.

I didn't know how I knew their language until I heard it. Stepping inside and closing the door behind me, I knelt to be near them. Yearning so close to their true selves, wanting to be their best versions—that I understood. But they weren't like the ax, which was a necessary tool for survival. These blades wanted death and power. This was wrong, profane, but I couldn't help myself.

The proper way to sharpen metal is to tell it stories. They have to be the kind metal likes, stories about bravery and love and sacrifice. As I whispered some faerie tales I knew, they grew, matured, sparkled. Their glass promises became crystalline realities. The closer I realized their vision, they less they needed me until they didn't need me at all. I'd shown them the way, and now I was spent. Helpless, I watched them swell and glisten, elongate and narrow to the finest edge forever, fulfilling their destiny of harm. Their screeches grew so loud it hurt my ears, terrified me.

I ran from the room to the farthest hospra on the Magistrate's property, ripping up that foolish apron Maw made me wear, leaving it in shreds on the ground. How that false sense of purpose had filled me and drained me just as quick left me sick. I never wanted to come here, to live among town folk, to sharpen knives for a bunch of men to make themselves feel stronger in a world they already controlled. I was half-tempted to climb the fence and disappear into the woods, but thought them town folk would brand me a witch for sure if I did. I fell asleep in the hospra pondering what to do next about those blades I had made my children.

The faded sweet perfume of a parfenia blossom clung to the air when I woke up. That surprised me, since it wasn't spring.

Nor did I see any petals, but they usually withered when the sun come up anyhow. The dumb cock had long since spoken. Groggy from parfenia-induced sleep, I climbed down from my hospra bed resolved. The knives had to listen to reason. They had to go back to what they had been. Then I'd tell Miss Ulna that it was beyond my powers to do what she wanted.

Finnas and his horses were already gone, and the rest of the estate was silent as an eclipse. Nor were there any sounds from my room. The knives were gone.

There would be no peace with my children loose like this. The compound gates were open, and I ran outside. The distant roar of a crowd told me why the streets were empty and where everybody was. Huffing, I made it to the edge of the crowd. The square was packed, and the Magistrate's cart was nowhere to be found. Slipping between people who never knew I existed, I could only get so far before people congealed around me. I heard the tiny chattering of the overeager knives, but couldn't figure where they were coming from.

On a platform in the middle of the square stood a tall, dark-haired woman with a rope draped around her neck and hands tied behind her back. Underneath the platform was a pile of firewood, as if hanging weren't permanent enough. Whatever she was accused of doing, it must have been so bad they wanted to kill her twice.

The crowd shushed, and I pushed forward looking for my unnatural creations. I didn't want my whispers to hurt anybody. Some folks were put off by my boldness and put up enough of a grumble that it caught Miss Ulna's attention from where she stood at the front of the mob. Rather than get mad, she gave me half a smile and put a finger to her lips. Makzeet and Trixa stood on either side of her, nodding when they saw me. In Trixa's hair was a pink parfenia blossom, impossibly preserved.

The Magistrate gimped the short distance to front of the platform. Townsmen crowded around him, shouting their support while hoisting axes and wheat scythes, bows and spears. None of their weapons talked to me, though I still heard the knives' faint voices.

Clearing his throat, the Magistrate puffed liked a bullfrog. "Sangela Terns of Stonefeld, you stand accused of foulness against the Maker. You have brought animality, wanton sensuality, and unnatural congress to our town. How do you plead before your fellow townsfolk?"

"I don't have to answer to anybody here."

The Magistrate harrumphed like this sort of outrageous response was beneath him. "Then I have no choice but to pronounce you guilty."

Sangela spit at the Magistrate, though she was too far away to reach him. She laughed when his puss soured and even more at the crowd's gasps and curses. Her hair collected itself into a ponytail, slunk across her shoulder and twitched like a cat's tail. Not just any cat, I saw now. Black and silky like it would glow in the moonlight, like it would waltz through the courtyard, like it would rub up against you and make you its friend.

"By official decree of the township of Stonefeld, I condemn you to death by hanging and burning." He made it sound more like a condition than a judgment.

Sangela only laughed louder. "Hanging and burning? Is that all?"

Some in the crowd guffed despite themselves. The Magistrate stumbled backward as if the words had been physical blows. He called his supporters to him. The knives hushed completely, like they were preparing to strike, and that scared me most.

"Enough. Men, ignite the pyre and drop the ropes by the common decree of Stonefeld and the Maker we serve."

As the men of Stonefeld came forward with their weapons and torches, I heard the voices of my children begin to sing as, one by one, the women of Stonefeld withdrew blades from under their aprons, the folds of their skirts, the hems of their gowns.

Miss Ulna unveiled one of largest and most violent of my pupils as she approached her husband, speaking so everyone could hear. "Harmon Fustable, your authority means no more to us than the fortunes told in the smatterings of pigeon droppings."

Before he could close his gaping mouth, she stabbed her husband in the belly. Overwhelmed and dumbstruck, his men had no immediate reaction. The other women didn't hesitate, and soon all I could hear was the screams of men, the shrieking laughter of women and the harmonic voices of my babies in their bloody glory. The Magistrate climbed the scaffolding behind the platform but was hunted by both Miss Ulna and Sangela. I couldn't watch them carve him up.

Some of the men put up their hands in surrender, and they were spared. Those who fought back didn't last long. There were too many women and too many knives. Whether or not anybody deserved this, I didn't know anymore. I hated bloodshed, killing, death, and felt sick that I had helped this happen. Miss Ulna, Makzeet, and Trixa had made me their fool. Maybe even Maw. None of them cared about me any more than the knives had at the end.

I hated tears but they came anyway as I ran from the massacre toward the town's gates. Howls followed me like accusations, pushing me forward through the panicking masses. Wiping my eyes, I headed toward those morbid city gates. They burst open as I approached, and I didn't dare look up.

Beyond a small gulley lay the forest, wild and lush. Maybe there I could find a way to forgive myself. I left the road as fast as my legs would take me, disappearing into the woods. The air chased me like a zephyr, batting me like a toy, lashing my back like a hiss.

See Matthew Amundsen's story "Country Whispers" online at Metaphorosis.

If you liked it, leave a comment. Authors love that!

Remember to subscribe to our e-mail updates so you'll know when new stories are posted.

About the story

I lived through a slightly different version of this story in a dream. The horrific ending stayed with me for quite a while, and only turning it into fiction could get it out of my mind. Translating a dream into fiction has its own pitfalls, but luckily I found a way to be true to the emotions of the dream as well as the character of Leusa.

A question for the author

Q: What is the first/most recent book that you lost sleep reading/thinking about?

A: The most recent book I lost sleep over was William S. Burroughs' *The Western Lands*. His reimagining of the Egyptian Book of the Dead was a dense and bittersweet coda to a long history of difficult works.

About the author

Matthew has lived in seven states and has worked in advertising, film and commercial production, and information management. He has been publishing fiction since 1990. When not writing, he is a musician and sound engineer in Minneapolis, where he lives with his daughter.

@gallopingfoxley

The Thousand Revolutions of Kronstadt

Pablo Valcarcel

Soon, the moment to die will come again. I do not look forward to it, but such is my duty to the revolution. For here, in the worker's paradise, we all must fight for the future: from the nurse to the soldier to the peasant. But while they all trudge in the darkness of the present, the Futurographer scouts ahead to find the hard reefs of his death and map the future for all others.

And yet, what good is the cartography of my deaths in the Becomingness if it's unable to spare my proletarian brothers and sisters? What good is being able to move swiftly through the dark chamber of uncertainty if we're ultimately trapped in a jail—or even worse, the slaughterhouse?

Tonight, I'm being sent into the violent rapids of our future once more, but this time, I'm not to predict the outcome of a battle, but rather to help suppress insurrection at my home in Kronstadt. In a telegram, the Secretary of War, Citizen Leon Trotsky himself, demanded names— no fewer than a hundred—of those enemies of the revolution to be put under arrest and hanged.

The idea revolts me. I have many friends among the sailors, and I know what they stand for. Until now, Kronstadt's sailors have been the Bolsheviks' watchdogs and the revolution's staunchest supporters. If they're about to revolt, it's not to sabotage revolution but rather to protect it. I know well that Ksana Vasilievna's name would be on that list, and the thought makes me queasy with dread. She's the one that started it all, but only because she was brave enough to come here to denounce the abuses in Petrograd.

When Dulkin, the head of the Cheka police in Kronstadt, came to me with the orders, I could have refused to help him, but that would have only made them question my own loyalty. Besides, if they're asking me this, it must be because another Futurographer in Moscow has seen this rebellion. I want to prevent this senseless bloodbath. And for that, I need to outsmart them all. I must see for myself what's to come.

This is why we're here: Misha and I, skulking about the lower deck of the battleship *Petropavlosk* like thieves in the night. Dulkin is here with us—he says that he's come to "protect us," but I reckon he's begun to suspect me. What else did that telegram say?

At least I have Misha to help me. He's my friend, but he's here tonight because I need him. He's the only electrician on board that I trust to operate the Futurography machine, and he's a member of the Communist party, so that makes Dulkin approve of him. Or so I hope.

In the cold of the Futurography chamber, I can see my breath loom in the air like a ghost. I can feel it too, seeping up from the frozen Baltic through the hull of the *Petropavlosk*. I can't really move, strapped as I am to the Chronosthesic engine, but I can squirm to fight it.

Misha continues working diligently, and soon the engine comes to life, powered by coal and oil. My whole body tingles with both dread and excitement as I try to clear my mind of any thoughts, opening it to the humming of the machine. But then the clanking of approaching footsteps on the stairs outside reminds me that we're still missing someone.

Misha cranes his head towards the closed door, and Dulkin reaches for his revolver.

"What did you tell the Firemen working the boilers, Anatoly Yuryevich?" Misha asks me in a low voice.

"Only that we were running some routine calibrations on the machine," I force a calmed smile. I need time, as much as I can have.

The footsteps veer away into the distance and they both relax, even though Dulkin keeps his hand on the holster.

"Hurry up! How long do you need, Futurographer Kolchunov?" asks Dulkin.

"How long can you hold your breath, Citizen Dulkin?" I reply.

Dulkin's eyes widen, and his grey, scrawny beard seems to part in a gaping crack of surprise. Misha chuckles softly, and I put on a coy smile. It's quite a thrill to see this man—one of the all-powerful Chekists, the secret police—watch me as dumbfoundedly as if I were a mystic.

"It is like diving in the ice out there, or at least it triggers a similar response in my body: less breathing, less circulation, until the brain finally runs out of oxygen. Anything more than ten minutes is risky, anything more than twenty will certainly cause cerebral damage. So fear not, there'll be time for a celebratory drink."

Dulkin titters and I laugh with him. It helps to ease the tension a bit.

Misha reads aloud the display of the equalisers as the machine warms. With my free hand, I adjust the chronograph on my left wrist to help me track the passing of the minutes: *February 28th, 1921. Elapsed travel time: 0 minutes.* The reason a Futurographer never removes his chronograph is that they're our compass in the Becomingness, marking both the current date and our time elapsed in the machine.

"Ready?" Misha asks.

I manage to move my chin in a slight gesture of assent. It's time.

"Good luck, Anatoly," he says.

"I'll see you soon."

Carefully, Misha raises the lever that opens the way for the electrical current to reach my cranium. A spark runs through my brain, lighting up my lethargic medial temporal lobe and flooding my head with endless fleeting images; the moment charges itself with an electrical effervescence.

My still body is held tightly by a dozen straps while my muscles contract in pain. As my perception breaks apart, a tingling sensation traverses my skin. It's as if my body were shifting around my mind, recomposing itself and feeding me disconnected flashes of information. And yet, despite my painful immobility, my mind leaps forward at an impossible speed.

I enter the Becomingness naked of thoughts. Still, it's difficult not to feel disoriented when my brain is flooded with waves of strange images and sensations. Even one's eyes seem strange when they're twisted by the tides of time. There is hardly time to understand or assimilate what I've seen before one image moves to the next, but from these fleeting encounters with my distorted reflections, shells of truth remain.

Stroke by stroke, I swim into the waters of the immediate future. There, I feel myself die often and rapidly. I discover a cluster of temporally close endings, a small island made up of a jumble of connected deaths. This might be exactly what I seek.

I fight to hold on to one wave. I cling to it and let soak me, engulf me. I must drown in it if I'm to understand.

March, 1921. Elapsed travel time: 2 minutes.

I suck in a mouthful of cold air before opening my eyes and checking my chronograph. I haven't drifted too far away in time. I'm standing on one of the battlements of the fortresses on the island of Kronstadt. The Baltic Sea is a frozen flatland of unending whiteness that lies at my feet, and its only wave is a legion of soldiers that march over the plains under the fire of our guns.

This is what I feared. Not only the sailor's bloody revolt but its suppression. And yet, somehow I'm decidedly on the side of the sailors. Why? Yes, they're my comrades, but so are the Red Army soldiers.

I've barely begun searching my own mind for the answers when an artillery barrage hits the wall, blowing the world apart around me. At full speed, I feel the vertigo of the fall turn into terror. Before my body smashes to pieces against the ice, I jump away, forcing my mind to detach itself from this current and seeking my next death. I focus on my body, the one that's trapped in the machine. It's there even if I can't feel it. I imagine my slow breathing, the unyielding cold, anything to shatter this illusion of death.

March, 1921. Elapsed travel time: 4 minutes.

My body convulses as I collide with a machine gun burst. I hit the ground, but what truly hurts are the gunshot wounds on my side and my left arm.

Around me, Kronstadt's white streets are littered with uniformed corpses. Within arm's reach, a comrade I don't recognise lies face down, his sailor's telnyashka shirt sown with lead and watered with blood.

Misha yells at me from a nearby alley. I try to gesture him away, but my muscles won't respond. Too late, he lurches forward in search of my fallen body. I always knew I could trust him with my life. In Kazan, when the Whites' bombs fell and hit the barge on which the Futurography machine was running, Misha pulled me out of the burning wreckage and took me ashore. Just like then, he runs towards me.

When he reaches my side, the Red Guards fire off their machine gun. The burst tears off half his mouth, and he falls by my side. He splatters me with his blood, like a muddy child playing with his friend. During those brief moments, whatever is left of his jaw opens and closes, trying to produce some sound. I manage to grab his arm, soaked in scarlet, trying to offer him some solace. Breathing has become difficult, and blood bubbles in my mouth. One of the bullets has pierced a lung.

This is a futile struggle. The sailors don't stand a chance against the might of the entire Red Army. *We* don't stand a chance. Still, I manage to move, propelled by deep anger. Despite the pain, I push myself upwards, every ounce of will against the gravity of my dying body. I only manage to kneel, but that's enough. Enough to wield my revolver and empty it against one of the soldiers handling the machine gun a few metres away. The young Red Army soldier falls dead instantly.

This is it. The end of the Soviet dream. Proletarian brother murdering Proletarian brother.

I drop my smoking weapon while a trickle of blood cascades down my mouth, warm and intoxicating. I'm too close to the end, too tightly held by its embrace. My entrails tremble with pain. I don't have the time to codify the memories from this life.

I need another stream, a different branch of my own history. Within the Becomingness, I graze through other oceanic currents:

There, I'm bleeding to death in Kronstadt, torn apart by rifle fire in the Anchor Square.

There, I suffocate in the fires of the Engineering School.

There, I'm shot against a white wall with other brother rebels.

But surely there is a way out of this. If not peace, at least escape? I swim away, I swim to a current that leaves the island.

Only in the workers' paradise, thanks to the geniuses of Citizens Pavlov and Theremin, have the volumes of time been pried open and mapped for the advancement of the revolution. With Theremin's Engine for Predictive Historical Materialism, a trained Futurographer can reveal a fraction of futures to come in the same way a chess player may project future positions on the board. But unlike the omniscient chess player, I can't see the entire board. I'm only a piece, a willing pawn—a knight perhaps—limited in awareness to his own moves. But in the right combination, my moves may reveal more.

Experiencing your final throes over and over is a strange sort of torture, but I have only myself to blame. Like a hunting dog, my mind has been trained to sniff out my own death and track it. It was Comrade Pavlov, the other father of Futurography, who theorised that one's death might act as a cartographic milestone. My endings are the reefs against which the swell of my time breaks, the shores on which my stream bleeds out roaring. Knowing them allows me to draw the shape of the seas we're to traverse in the future.

But how many deaths can a mind experience without falling apart? During our hasty training at Comrade Ioffe's Institute in Petrograd, the majority of my class quit before they completed their training. It is telling that they would prefer to go back to the frontlines to fight the Whites rather than lose their sanity.

Of those of us who didn't abandon their studies, the majority succumbed to chronosthesic delirium. I remember some of them being dragged away from the machine, forever lost into a state of vegetative idiocy. I also remember a friend, a young Ukranian engineer, forever possessed by constant hysterical attacks and atemporal ravings.

Not many of us were spared. And then we were taken to the front and employed to predict Admiral Kolchak's battle plans and actions. We helped to turn the tide at the direst hour in Kazan and saved uncountable lives. But at what cost?

Somehow I survived it all with only some shrapnel in my left leg and a few horrible images locked in my mind, but my fellow Futurographers were not so lucky. I was among the few to remain in active service, assigned to Kronstadt. How was I different from my comrades? Was it my fondness for chess and calculating possible scenarios? Or was my mind singularly shaped to cope with death?

If anything spared my mind from decay, it was my blind love for the revolution, my desperate hope that there was a purpose to all this suffering. A justification, a final utopia waiting for us at the end of the road. Predictive Materialism is a scientific discipline, but it does require a sort of faith: an unbreakable certainty that there will be a better tomorrow that justifies the tribulations we're faced with now.

March, 1921. Elapsed travel time: 7 minutes.

In the darkness of the night, I stop, panting, and check the chronograph before resuming our desperate flight from the Bolsheviks through the frozen plain that separates us from Finland. By my side, several sailors advance, armed with their rifles, bags, blankets, and whatever little else they've been able to hastily salvage from the city. Cold and fatigue gnaw at both our skin and the muscles beneath it. When I turn, I see her, a woman laden with heavy filming equipment. In fact, with the same camera that started it all.

She trudges ahead, but there's a stubborn grace to her. Perhaps it's because of her distinguished bearing and features, or her auburn hair, messy and wild. When one of her film cases falls to the ground and rolls away, she stops.

After considering, I drop my rifle and run to her aid. I help her pick it up and then, a lone bullet hits me in the leg. I bite back a curse. The pursuing soldiers are almost upon us.

"Take your camera and run, Ksana!"

"Anatoly!" she responds, gripping her camera tightly but hesitating over me.

"Go, please! You need to show them everything!"

She mouths something I can't hear, an apology perhaps, or a goodbye—still, she doesn't waver, and bolts away.

The bullet must have cut through an artery, for I'm bleeding out quickly. We were fleeing, but where to? It doesn't really matter. This Anatoly cares for her enough to try to escape with her from the fighting in Kronstadt.

I step back into the Becomingness, tracing other currents running in parallel. There aren't many. I seem to perish far more often than not in the rebellion. But if I escape, it seems to be with her. How come she suddenly means so much to me?

I still remember when she arrived on the island. Many scoffed at her, an idealistic member of the intelligentsia among the rough sailors, but I saw more than that. Behind her two shining blue irises, I saw the revolution in flesh and bone: a new world in which our comrades, proletarian women, have opportunities beyond the labour of the fields, the work at the factories, or the raising of a family.

When she tried showing us her reels from Petrograd, nobody took her seriously at first. The city is not even a day away; certainly we knew what was happening there. But then we *saw* it all.

We saw workers of all kinds, from the steel factories to the tobacco plants, protesting in the streets. We saw the army dispersing them with gunfire. We saw soldiers forcing those same workers to remain in their posts at gunpoint. Her reels were an eye-opening mirror, one that showed a Petrograd very much like the one we had liberated from the Tsar.

The old Tsar might be dead, but still the people starved and died by the hand of the army. It didn't matter that the Bolsheviks were wielding the weapons, the workers were the ones wounded. "A few moving pictures aren't the truth," the Bolshevik Commissar on the island said, but it was too late. Those moving pictures had lit a fuse, and the whole naval base was aflame. In just a matter of hours, the sailors, until then some of the staunchest watchdogs of Communism, were loudly denouncing its abuses.

I spent hours debating with Ksana Vasilievna. She argued the need for immediate change, while I defended the necessity of a long term view. I spoke in favour of predictive materialism and of Futurography to show us the way and on strong leadership to bring forth that vision. She countered saying that no future could be conquered without gaining a foothold in the hearts and minds of today's women and men.

And yet, what I remember most is her smile and the contagious wonder in her words as if she were a storyteller sharing a captivating fairytale instead of outlining the principles of a new world. Was it then that I began to care for her? Possibly. But when did I start to care for her more than I've ever cared for the revolution?

I reject this notion. All these years, I've lived and died to serve the revolution. I've known no love other than my faith in our future, no family other than my brother sailors.

Mine is an agnostic and empirical love to the cause. A thousand times over, I've seen what it will do to me, and still, I believe that we'll make a better world. My only devotion is to the incandescent truths born in the darkness of the Futurography chamber.

What does my own happiness matter when compared to the freedom of the people? Though when I stop to consider... why have I been forced to choose?

I can see the rebellion of the sailors ending in a furious bloodbath one way or another, but this is not an answer. I must go deeper in time.

I know that a Futurographical journey of such magnitude is a reckless endeavour. All those I knew who attempted it died or were committed because of chronosthesic delirium. Their brains collapsed under the sheer volume of raw information or decayed because of the time spent in the machine.

And yet I must try.

How could I abandon the sailors, Misha, and Ksana Vasilievna to die? I must find answers. I must find a way out for us all.

Furiously, I swim forward, trying not to let the stream pull me too far, but the current is far stronger than I had anticipated. It pushes me with the strength of a tempest.

October, 1925. Elapsed travel time: Uncertain. 9 minutes (estimated).

We're making our way through the thick snow in the middle of a Siberian blizzard. The wind lashes at us angrily through our prisoners' uniforms, little more than soaked rags. In this wave, they've taken my chronograph from me, so I'm forced to count the seconds mentally.

Misha is helping me carry a heavy beam. Even here, in this grim place crafted to break the human spirit, he is a brother to me. But there's not much left of me, or him for that matter; we're both dregs of the revolution. Refuse left behind by the purges, and then vomited into this frozen graveyard.

I skim through my memories quickly, trying to understand whether this is a result of the Kronstadt rebellion, but the truth is worse than that: even remaining faithful to the Bolsheviks, we've been sent to a gulag. Comrade Stalin and his ilk despise us; they've deemed Futurography a threat too big for the party.

Intense dizziness hits me. My nose bleeds and my lungs burn, but the worst thing is my heart. Worn out after years of wasting away in this work-camp, each step I take forward is a colossal struggle. My arms begin shaking.

"Hold on, Anatoly! Just a little longer!" Misha yells.

But my arms won't listen, and I let go of my side of the beam. Misha curses, but I can't even apologise. I collapse on the snow, breathing heavily as pain fills my chest.

He rushes towards me, and his gaunt, bearded face creates a stark outline against the shifting whiteness of the skies.

I try uttering some words; I want him to know how sorry I am for abandoning him to his fate. But he can't hear me under the wailing winds.

He holds my hand as pain tears through my heart like a bullet. I can't stay in the machine much longer without risking neuronal damage. I clench my teeth and leap onto a nearby wave in the Becomingness.

June, 1927. Elapsed travel time: 11 minutes (est.).

I'm atop a scaffold at the centre of St. Vasily's Descent in Moscow. My neck is tightly wrapped in a rough noose, warm in the cold evening's breeze.

I'm not alone. I share the scaffold with other Futurographers. Citizen Theremin isn't among us; he's fled to America, or so they say. A quiet crowd has gathered to watch us die. There's more of them than I'd have anticipated, but they keep a respectful silence. I search for familiar faces among them, but the grey and chapped countenances all look the same from here.

They don't even seem all human. They are hollow beings, devoured by a hunger born from years of famine and scarcity. A hunger so deep that it's eaten every single one of the dreams they once held inside themselves.

Someone else from Kronstadt is here with us: Citizen Dulkin reads aloud a summary of our trial, including our signed confessions of having betrayed the Proletariat by offering false reports to the party. "They've wilfully misguided the Party! They've sabotaged the economic planning and brought us famine and poverty!"

He's lying. They've ignored our reports over and over, because hunger is a tool for them. The Bolsheviks have swallowed the revolution and turned it into a grim masquerade. Prisoners turn into frozen skeletons in the depths of the gulags. Shooting squads play the music of their guns for blindfolded audiences. And we, the hanged men, dance for the crowds in public squares. They've turned the revolution into a melting furnace where we're all to be remade to the image of the party.

"Behold, comrades! This is the fate reserved to all who defy the dictatorship of the Proletariat! To all those who dare threaten the glorious future the party has built for us!"

"We'll see each other again, Citizen Dulkin," I say defiantly, but my voice is cracked.

Dulkin looks at me with hatred and kicks the stool from beneath my feet. I plummet towards my death. As the blood begins clogging my head and I lurch with my dangling legs, I push myself out.

August, 1928. Elapsed travel time: 13 minutes (est.).

I open my eyes to a blurry image of white and red. It's difficult to breathe and my heart hurts with a burning sensation, but I force my eyes wide open.

I'm tied to a chair, head leaning over my chest, facing a cellar floor of immaculate tiles stained by a mosaic of blood drops. My legs radiate in excruciating waves of pain, but even so, it takes me a while to recognise those two grotesque sculptures of purplish meat for what they are: they are what's left of my feet, ankles, and knees.

Dulkin is seated by my side. His uniform is crumpled, and there are deep shadows underneath his eyes. His revolver rests on his lap, and he's leaning back in his chair, waiting for a cigarette to die in my lips. In the chilly air of the room, the smoke of my cigarette floats like a playful ghost. Am I in the Cheka prison in Moscow? Or is this the one in Kronstadt? The memories of different purges dance in my mind, mingling and shifting.

"It was always bound to end like this, Anatoly, don't you see? Communism, our glorious future, is unstoppable. It's bigger than you or me. Before the revolution, history was a locomotive out of control, one bound to crash and drag us all with it, but now the party will lay the tracks in the right direction. Perhaps the Patriarchs weren't wrong after all. Man is flawed and needs a perfect and omnipotent God to rule over it. But that is the party, is it not?"

What does he want from me? To beg? Or is it to reassure him? I inhale one last time and then let the butt fall to my lap. When it touches me, I only feel a distant burn, incapable of disrupting the serenity that fills me around the agony of my legs.

I manage to croak a reply: "Who are you trying to convince, Dulkin, me or yourself?"

He leans forward as if eager to share a confidence.

"You think yourself better than me, Kolchunov? You think you're the only one who isn't blinded by the illusion of time? You think that you can swim away to another "wave" to escape this? Well, here's the truth for you, Anatoly: all waves are headed in the same direction. With Comrade Trotsky at the helm, we'll use Futurography to steer the world towards the utopia. Who cares if you think that your vision for the future is different? It means nothing in the grand scheme of things. Your voice means nothing."

"And yours does?"

"Neither does mine. The collective will of the Proletariat is absolute, don't you understand? Change and revolution are for the many, for every single Proletarian of the world! The future too belongs to the collective... And for the revolution to triumph, for us to defeat Imperialistic Capitalism and bourgeoisie democracy, we must eliminate any dissidence!"

"Dissidence and liberty..."

He's sweating now, agitated: "What don't you understand? Individual liberty is dissidence! Liberty is an illusion. That was never the struggle! None of us can be truly free until we're all free... If only you had seen this! There's still time for you to help us, Anatoly. To help us steer the future together with the party."

"Keep saying that to yourself."

"A man matters nothing, Anatoly! Even if he's a Futurographer! Tell me that I'm wrong! Tell me that you've seen different."

"You can't quench human thirst for freedom."

"Perhaps. But we can quell rebellion, as we did with the sailors."

"I am still here, am I not?"

"No. You're wrong. You're not. I will hunt and kill you as many times as it's necessary, Kolchunov."

He places the barrel of his gun to my temple, and I swim away before the discharge.

He can't be right. His mind is too narrow, his eyes too small to contain the potential of the revolution. Humanity's yearning for freedom is far larger than this, thus the revolution must be more than this. It *must* be.

I swim through the pain:

There, my heart is giving up in the middle of torture in the Cheka's dungeons.

There, I'm dancing the hangman's dance once more in Petrograd.

There, my very marrow freezes in the cruel Siberian winter.

I want to prove him wrong. But my time has already run out, and the deeper I enter the Becomingness, the more dire the prospects seem. Still, I have to find an answer—I have to find a spark of hope. Some proof that this isn't it all doomed: the revolution, the unrest in Petrograd and Kronstadt... Humanity's dream of liberty.

Somewhere in my past, my body begins convulsing. I ignore it. I force myself to keep searching, to venture the farthest I've ever been, despite the length of time I've spent in the machine, despite the decaying of my mind.

I sink into a turbulent ocean of rapid and violent currents. A hundred blurry endings slip slowly through my throat like razors, drowning me in my own blood. Even catching glimpses of them hurts.

There, I am running through Berlin's crowded streets when they finally shoot me in the back.

There, I'm trudging through Chicago's blasted concrete landscape when I step on a mine.

I wish I could flee, return to my warm flesh, to the blindness of immediacy. But I can't. This is who I am. I've lived for this future, for the foolish promise that humanity would grow wiser.

Instead, there's an island, an entire continent of war and destruction ahead of me. It stretches in every direction, a global war that devours the world. I die over and over again, in Trotskygrad, London, Amsterdam, a thousand deaths for the revolution. Is this the price of world revolution? Will the world be remade into paradise through another Great War?

And then I find a gnawing hole in the ocean, a trench into which lives fall and becomes nothingness. Somehow, time itself runs dry. Somehow, the future has devised weapons and horrors capable of putting an end to everything.

The hole sucks me in, but I fight it with every bit of strength left in me. It's not courage but fear that possesses me. I swim backwards, reeling in horror. I force myself to ignore the cold of millions of images burning through my closed eyelids in rapid succession. I push back through huge waves of time, entire lives, joyous and miserable, yet to be lived. But all for what? Perhaps I deserve to die here. Perhaps this is my punishment.

I gain some distance from the maelstrom but at a great cost. I'm now too spent, and I've lost my bearing. When a wave hits me from behind, I'm too weak to resist it and it traps me in its grasp.

May, 1937. Elapsed travel time: 19 minutes (est.).

I'm standing at the end of a pier in Barcelona's harbour. This sea is foreign to me, its deep blue waters nothing like the Baltic's charcoal grey. A salty wind runs over the docks, mixed with the toasted afternoon air. But I can't quite enjoy the scene. Even if this country is at war, even though I'm a soldier, I'm an outcast, a sombre stain in the human landscape of this city.

But I'm not alone in this solitude. Ksana Vasilievna is curled up against my chest, as if she prefers the sound of my heart to the rumour of the waves. Here, she isn't Citizen Shatunova anymore, but just Ksana. I can see the passing of the years in the premature wrinkles of her face, but she still has the same brilliant eyes. Not only is she still beautiful, but now she carries the gravitas of someone who has seen whole cities dissolve like sand castles with the tide.

Soon they'll come for us. Spain is having its own war, but also its own revolution. Anarchists and Socialists are remaking society here, and yet they're hunted, not just by the Fascists but also by the Bolsheviks.

Even here, the Cheka will make sure that only the Bolsheviks can craft the future of the revolution. They'll purge the Spanish Anarchists if they must, and they'll certainly execute two self-exiled traitors like us. We could have hidden somewhere else, but Ksana didn't want to. Even facing death, she isn't afraid.

She came, and I followed. Here, she's fought for revolution and change in the only way she knows: with words and images. With her reels from Kronstadt and other places. With her truths about our victories and our failings. For the revolution is never done, and never right, and she helps birth it over and over again, with truth and inspiration.

Ksana stops me when she sees me examining the chronograph. She reaches for my face and forces me to meet her eyes.

"Is it time, my love? Well then, Anatoly, I need you to remember this. Even if it doesn't end like one of Pushkin's fairy tales, this moment matters. You and I, and this moment, we all matter. There are fires that can never be extinguished. Just like us."

Then she stands on her tiptoes and places a deep kiss on my lips. A spark burns within my heart. The emotion reaches me cushioned, just like the sound of bullets through the waters in Kazan, but even so it hits the mark.

I can feel the gravitational pulse of this time, of her and our shared journey. Why would I want to return to Kronstadt's cold and hunger, rather than remain here by her side? If only I could remain here! This must be the root for cronosthesic delirium: getting lost on some island of the future like a castaway. If I stay with her, my heart will collapse, while my brain makes a futile attempt to to codify a whole life yet to be lived. And yet, even knowing that, I'm tempted, drawn to her and this moment.

The spell breaks when we hear a group of men approaching us. The few scrawny fishermen and children around us scatter away as soon as they see the weapons. They'd be even more scared if they recognised the man leading them.

"At last, *camaradas*!" Dulkin calls to us. "I feared that you might have left the city already. Luckily, there's still time for a proper farewell."

He addresses those accompanying him in Spanish. I don't need to hear him to tell what he's saying. As the Chekists raise their guns, I hug Ksana and shield her with my body.

"Don't worry, love. I won't forget."

We kiss, and their fusillade pierces my back, bullets cutting through ribs and lungs. For once, the hardest part isn't dying, but rather letting her go.

I have in me a final stroke, but not much more. I want to return home, to life. But now more than ever do I want to prevent this senseless bloodbath.

With one last effort, I push myself back towards the point of origin. Nausea pinches at the bottom of my stomach, the waves striking me until I catch a slow one.

I sink into it, soak myself in it. I let it infect every skin pore, permeate every sensory detail. I drown in it.

Ksana's face is the first thing I see when I open my eyes. She's holding a wet cloth against my forehead.

"He's awake!" she calls out.

My face is covered in sweat, and I have trouble breathing. My nostrils are inundated with the sticky aroma of blood. When I search around, I realise I'm lying on the floor of the Futurography chamber and that the room seems to have been seized by armed sailors. Some have Misha and Dulkin pinned against the wall. Ksana Vasilievna seems to be leading them.

They all stutter at different speeds, as my mind struggles to synchronise itself with the present.

"For a moment I thought you had died on me. But it turns out that you were just sleeping, just like—"

"The princess in Pushkin's tale," I manage to interject.

"Yes! The dead Princess and the seven knights... But how?" Her bright eyes narrow. She must understand, or intuit what I've seen.

"Enough! Tell us, what's happening here?" The man addressing me is one of the leaders among the sailors, a dark-moustached fireman that holds the barrel of his gun firmly against Misha's chest.

"They've been planning to arrest and kill us all!" some scrawny blond sailor calls from the back. "I told you that the Bolsheviks wouldn't let us protest peacefully!"

"You're damn right about that!" boasts Dulkin. "We'll never give away power, for such is our duty to the revolution. Surrender your weapons now, and I assure you that your rebellion will be forgiven!"

His little speech is interrupted when someone punches him. Soon, another blow follows, and some other sailor hits Misha with the butt of his rifle. "Let's kill these Chekists!" someone yells, and I can see the young blond sailor point his rifle at me.

Ksana Vasilievna rises to stop them with her arms outstretched. For a moment, I fear she too might be struck down, but the sailor backs off.

"Let him speak! He's risked his life to find what awaits us. He's the only one who can tell us whether rebelling against the Bolshevik rule will accomplish anything!" she yells.

The sailors seem to hesitate, but the coaler turns to address her: "You want us to trust a Chekist?"

"Anatoly Yuryevich is a Futurographer, but he isn't a Chekist. In fact, he's the one who told me about this experiment he was doing. He wanted me here to witness it, to film it for all of us. He loves the revolution like us." She turns to face me, and her confusion has shifted into something else: fear, but also a strange recognition. "He has my trust."

The fireman slowly gives in. "Very well, speak then! What did you see, Futurographer?"

Ksana turns on her phonograph, and all of the sudden, my throat is dry. "Tell us, Comrade," Ksana beseeches me. "Tell everyone what you saw." Everyone's eyes are on me. Those of the sailors gleam with renewed hopes. Am I willing to smash their dreams? To tell them that they will most likely fail? Dulkin offers me a crooked smile, certain of his hold on things. Am I ready to denounce the Party and sign my own death warrant?

I could craft the right lie to avoid it all. Something pleasant to appease both sides, a tale to buy us some time and allow Misha and I to escape the island before it all goes to hell. We could steal some horses and ride all the way to Finland. Run away before it's too late.

But I can see in Ksana's eyes that it wouldn't be enough for her. As if she can feel my doubts, she speaks: "Comrade Kolchunov—Anatoly, just give us the truth. It's the only thing we want."

So I tell them.

I tell them everything. I speak both of the terrible purges and the doomed rebellion. I tell them how the revolution is to become an inhospitable country, a mother that devours its children, a war waged on the present in the name of a future that will never arrive. A future so perfect and pure that it shall never touch us. An idea that will just loom, admitting no compromise, no concession. On its name, the Bolsheviks shall make righteous all sacrifices and atrocities. On its name, all liberties will be postponed, all voices made one.

But history can be remade. In fact, I tell them, it is now being remade in front of my eyes. In Kronstadt, the voice of the revolution has been returned to the throats of the people. The present belongs to them, and only to them. Life is no longer to be postponed; it now must be lived.

The Bolsheviks might unleash the mighty fury of the Red Army to kill us all, but they can't prevent us from lighting a beacon.

And then, as if to punctuate my words, a shot explodes in the room.

I'm lying on the floor looking upwards, a bullet wound burning in my side. Dulkin struggles as they take his revolver, but he still manages to scream at me as they drag him away: "How much gold have they promised you for your lies, Kolchunov? You're nothing but traitorous Tsarist scum! You shall pay for all these lies!"

This is the final nail in their coffin. The Bolsheviks have already lost control of Kronstadt, the sailors will rebel, and their fire will be seen through the ages. These people fear neither the Bolshevik's wrath, nor the other dented reefs of Becomingness. Their hearts are swollen with a timeless love for liberty. And this is the only compass that will ever guide them.

I'm bleeding and my vision is blurry, but I manage to see Misha persuade the sailors to let him run to fetch a doctor. Then, Ksana kneels by my side and places her hands over mine, helping me put pressure on the wound.

I know death, the final destination of all of my journeys. And yet, despite our familiarity, I reject it. I cling to these seconds and this burning breath. Right now life feels more than a fleeting dream of the Futurography chamber. It is a fraction of infinity waiting to be conquered. It must be seized, the momentary must be made momentous.

Thus I look at Ksana, and, much to my delight, she meets my gaze with the same eyes she had for me in Spain. The same spark that will make us boundless together.

See Pablo Valcárcel's story "The Thousand Revolutions of Kronstadt" online at Metaphorosis.
If you liked it, leave a comment. Authors love

that!
Remember to subscribe to our e-mail updates so you'll know when new stories are posted.

About the story

The story of Kronstadt's ill-fated rebellion is one I've been fascinated with for a few years now. Since I first read about it, it struck me as being the pivotal moment in the Soviet Revolution, one signaling the abandonment of a lot of the revolution's idealism.

One can't help but to wonder whether Soviet Russia would be a very different country had they succeeded. Sadly, as it is, it only served as a grim prelude to what most anarchist revolutions would undergo during the rest of the 20th Century (e.g. The purging of Anarchists by Communists during the Spanish Civil war comes to mind).

Beyond the historical facts, another seed that helped to spring this tale into being was Boris Pasternak's classic *Doctor Zhivago*. Not only does Pasternak pull off a compelling love story with the revolution as a backdrop, but I must thank him for the inspiration regarding one of the central themes of my story (i.e. 'Life isn't to be postponed').

The final inspiration comes from the German Neofolk band Rome. It was their poetic-musical piece "The Chronicles of Kronstadt" that sparked the idea for the Futurographer's grim cartographical approach of using their own deaths as milestones.

A question for the author

Q: What are you reading now?

A: Currently, I'm reading Gareth Hanrahan's excellent debut *The Gutter Prayer*. It feels very fresh to me, and kind of reminds me of the first time I read China Miéville's *Perdido Street Station*. Both are urban fantasy tales set in labyrinthine cities, and both have some really fascinating worldbuilding behind them. Other fresh reads in my mind are Erin Morgenstern's *The Night Circus* and Stanislaw Lem's *Solaris*. *The Night Circus* was a delightful read. It offered plenty of dreamlike, romantic vistas wrapped up in exquisite prose. Lem's *Solaris*, on the other hand, ended being up a much harder read for me, but at the same time, the power of its imagery and its philosophical ideas made the journey completely worth it.

About the author

Pablo Valcárcel is based in Madrid where he teaches entrepreneurship, mentors startups and writes speculative fiction. You can follow his musings on mortality, Scrum for writers, and haunting songs on Twitter @awakedreamer.

Las Vegas Museum of Space Exploration

Marilee Dahlman

MISSION & HOURS

The purpose of the Las Vegas Museum of Space Exploration is to preserve and display extraterrestrial art and material of incredible cultural importance: the Mars Frescoes and Earth's largest collection of MarsBlood.

> Monday-Saturday except holidays
> 10am-5pm (security considerations may change hours)
> Timed Entry Only; Self-Guided Tours No Longer Permitted
> Gift shop closed until further notice.

GUIDE TO THE MUSEUM

Welcome! Rest assured that your safety is our top priority. Thank you for visiting the finest museum in Las Vegas. Our innovative architecture has won international acclaim, and our exhibits are out of this world! A little history:

The Man. Businessman, philanthropist and explorer Rupert A. Hammer III built this world-class museum. Mr. Hammer famously said, "I bet on red and I won." The red he was referring to was, of course, the planet Mars.

After trumped-up human trafficking allegations cut short a promising political career, Mr. Hammer turned his attention to legitimate off-planet business endeavors. The year was 2060. An international coalition was colonizing the asteroid Ceres to serve as a steppingstone to Jupiter's moon Europa. Mars was not considered a desirable target for new discoveries or exploitation.

Enter Mr. Hammer. He uniquely saw financial potential in the red planet. He built the fastest freight spacecraft ever made, and responsible government officials awarded him a contract to ship equipment and workers to the growing colony on Ceres. Hammer predicted that his interplanetary shipping venture would break even after his first delivery and become profitable thereafter. Plus, he had another plan to generate revenue: on each return trip, he would stop at Mars and fill his empty cargo holds with something—anything—that might sell on Earth. Ever the perceptive businessman, he reasoned, "If people will pay thousands for a gram of moon dust, what would they pay for a pound of Mars rock?" Scientists had already studied the planet's geology and warned that there was nothing worth the expense of hauling to Earth in great quantities. Hammer ignored the naysayers.

Using discarded mining equipment that had functioned sub-optimally on asteroid rock, Mr. Hammer blasted out a quarry on the softer surface of Mars. They say that fortune favors the bold, and that certainly happened here. Hammer discovered a strange material that would, quite conveniently, be highly economical to ship: an extraordinarily light, iron and magnesium-rich mineral that possessed a sponge-like molecular structure less than 1% the density of steel but twenty times as strong. It was pink-colored and malleable, much like Earth-based clay.

Manufacturing conglomerates, scientific research organizations, and various governments subsidized Hammer's subsequent journeys in exchange for mineral samples. Hammer hired an army of attorneys to maintain a monopoly in the ore, which was justified, given the risk and expense of his efforts. The potential applications for the new mineral ran the spectrum from spacecraft design to dental fillings.

Experts disagreed on the origin of the material and even its existing composition and structure. Some theorized that its molecular structure shouldn't be considered rock at all, and was, in fact, akin to the complex fibers of Earth-based natural spider silk.

At a plant near the Nevada Commercial Craft landing zone, Hammer fired the Mars clay into uniform-sized bricks. Each brick retained an incredible strength-to-weight ratio and gleamed a lustrous red without need for any paint. Hammer marketed them as 'MarsBlocks' for use in urban construction. Public demand was insatiable for such rare, beautiful, and practical extraterrestrial building material. Hammer focused sales in Las Vegas and set premium prices. This city had an ideal mix of wealthy and tasteful consumers, proximity to the brick factory, and flexible building ordinances.

The Discovery. In 2072, on Mr. Hammer's third trip to Mars, he made the greatest discovery of all time: the Mars Frescoes. Beneath the surface of the planet, Hammer a discovered a cave with hieroglyphics on the smooth pink walls. The images depicted nude women bathing in a vivid red stream. They were humanoid women, with bodies similar to ours, each with a head, limbs, eyes, nose and mouth. But they were alien, too. Their eyes and ears were significantly larger than ours. They had seven-fingered hands and long, fluid limbs. Their facial expressions were pleasant. Hammer personally funded the preservation of this glorious art and has made it accessible to all on Earth.

At first, many questioned the authenticity of Mr. Hammer's find. Subsequent events erased all doubt that this explorer had discovered true evidence of alien life. Some suggested that Hammer stop MarsBlock production until his discovery could be fully investigated. He boldly continued and proclaimed, "development is our destiny." Mr. Hammer spent the next fifteen years excavating the Mars Frescoes, delivering them safely to Las Vegas, and producing MarsBlocks in ever-increasing quantities. He built a futuristic castle-home in the desert constructed almost entirely of MarsBlocks. He began construction of the Hammer Interstellar Hotel & Casino on the Strip, also using MarsBlocks.

Demand stayed high. MarsBlocks became a common feature of Las Vegas residential and commercial construction, including many space-themed restaurants, casinos, bars and nightclubs. Hammer donated MarsBlocks for a new professional soccer stadium. Las Vegas was affectionately nicknamed Mars City.

The Aftermath. To this day, no one knows why the oozing began. The phenomenon gained widespread attention when Hammer did a live online tour of his new MarsBlock three-story pool cabana. A red drop splattered on his bare shoulder. He calmly transferred his cigar to his other hand and wiped off the red substance, looking up at the ceiling in surprise. It was a moment replicated in countless ways across the city. MarsBlock walls, floors, ceilings, staircases, counters —all parts of construction, in all types of buildings—began, very slowly, to melt. It didn't seem caused by a simple change in temperature. The resulting red liquid wasn't corrosive or harmful. But it didn't evaporate, seep into the ground, dry up into flakes, or otherwise disappear. The liquid seems attracted to itself. Often, two nearby red pools will thin and spread out until they connect. Eventually, the substance briefly re-hardens into slabs, and liquefies again. To date, the best scientists have not identified what triggers these cyclical changes in form. Most agree that with each cycle, the substance's molecular structure becomes slightly more complex.

Tourism suffered somewhat. The globby red liquid became known as MarsBlood. Hammer's castle-home and large sections of Las Vegas dripped down. The sticky substance formed large, thick pools around the city, from the Strip to the suburbs, and the National Guard closed streets and performed evacuations. Hammer's financial empire teetered on the brink of disaster.

MarsBlood looked unclean and many were disgusted by it or even afraid. It smelled metallic and had the texture of melting candle wax. Some animals and daring humans tried drinking it, and it wasn't too harmful in small amounts unless the stagnant, thick liquid was infected with Earth-based harmful bacteria. In some respects, it may be healthy. Plants growing near it seem to flourish. Animals are attracted to it, and dogs, in particular, will sit contently near a pool of MarsBlood for hours and protect it. Experts continue to analyze for any sign that the MarsBlood itself may be some kind of intelligent life. Obviously, there is a lot we don't understand. The smartest people in the world are working day and night to unlock the secrets of MarsBlood.

Mr. Hammer faced significant public pressure to address the crisis. He rose to the occasion. His first idea involved delivering huge amounts of sand and cotton to soak up the MarsBlood at the Hammer Interstellar Hotel & Casino and Hammer Interstellar Stadium construction sites. It didn't work. At its worst stage, an astronaut commented that from space, "the lovely blue marble Earth looks like it has a popped, bleeding zit in area of Vegas."

The Solution. You are standing inside the sublime resolution to the crisis. A soaring, some say cathedral-like, ruby-red museum built with collected MarsBlood. This is a collaborative public and private space designed to implement a policy of respectful containment. Government inspectors assess its safety on a daily basis.

Originally Mr. Hammer's idea, this is how it works: trained experts pour MarsBlood inside specially designed glass cubes. Each cube, a uniform thirty centimeters on each side, has exterior layers of laminated glass strong enough to repel bullets and withstand earthquakes and tornadoes. The inner layer is an ultra-thin, flexible glass that allows sufficient empty space for the MarsBlood's periodic transition to solid form. Each resulting glass container is a brilliant crimson MarsCube. MarsCubes, along with concrete and steel supports, form the walls, floors, ceilings and stairs of this stunning and structurally sound twenty-story museum.

The Future. What's in store for MarsBlood, and ourselves? From the desk of Mr. Hammer himself:

Make no mistake, I believe the rumors about the MarsBlood hands. I've seen one myself. One day, not long ago, I was sitting in my top floor museum office, where I keep a prototype MarsCube. Before my eyes, the red liquid formed a hand. Its seven fingertips briefly pressed against the glass and dissolved back into formless liquid. Some say that such a hand wants to be free. Remember this—no matter how exquisite, a hand can always close into a fist or wrap around a neck. Perhaps the MarsBlood's mesmerizing, red-apple sheen may itself be an aggressive trait, much like the brightly-colored lure of a predatory plant.

We don't know everything about MarsBlood, but we do know ourselves. As human beings, it is our nature to be assertive, inquisitive and industrious; therefore, development—not just discovery —is our destiny. Now we face something greater than destiny. This is about survival. Some argue that if MarsBlood births into an intelligent, humanoid life in the state of Nevada, the being(s) would have constitutional rights of citizenship. Some want MarsCubes transported to the desert (or even all the way back to Mars!) and emptied in order to allow the MarsBlood to unite and evolve freely.

I disagree! I believe, like many others, that we should put our safety first. Let scientists have more time to analyze the substance. It seems that MarsBlood has no 'MarsBrain,' or at least won't for quite some time. If it has no brain, it can have no consciousness or emotion. A 4x4 wood beam was once part of a living tree; do we attribute feelings to it? The MarsCubes are a perfect, sensible solution to allow all of us to view alien life. At the present time, layers of bulletproof glass contain the MarsBlood in a safe, respectful manner. And my solution supports the interest of transparency. All of us, for the price of a plane ticket (Hammer Interstellar Hotel offers excellent hotel/flight packages) get to participate in this journey of discovery. What will happen next? If not for the MarsCube, how long would it have taken to learn that the MarsBlood has concentric whorl fingerprints? Would our own government have told us, or not?

I am happy to announce development of an elegant super-cube that would provide more space for the MarsBlood to evolve into whatever it wishes. If there is enough popular demand, I could unveil the new super-cube as early as next year! Rest assured, I will fight all efforts to close down this museum. Our collective exploration and understanding of our neighbor, the beautiful red planet, has only just begun.

SIGNATURE EXHIBIT – RULES AND GUIDELINES

The Mars Frescos are located in the Atrium of Adventure, directly ahead. What we ask:

- Be respectful. We don't understand life in all its forms. Keep in mind that MarsBlood may be a living being.
- We discourage touching the glass and use of flash photography in case such actions disturb the MarsBlood in some way we don't understand.
- Do not attempt to break or vandalize the glass, as the MarsCubes function as an integral part of the museum's building structure.
- Notify a museum employee promptly if you see any sign of a MarsCube leak. Keep entrance and exit doors closed in order to help us keep dogs and rodents off the premises.

- Armed private security patrols the museum at all times. Special Forces units assigned by the United States Army are on 24/7/365 stand-by to respond to any emergency. Pulling an alarm as a prank is subject to prosecution.
- The U.S. Mars Research & Defense Facility is located adjacent to the museum. It is absolutely off-limits. To reach Las Vegas Boulevard from the Atrium of Adventure, simply exit through the MarsCube Skyway. Do not attempt to enter any museum room marked 'Authorized Personnel Only.'

Thank you for your cooperation. Please show your museum ticket at the Hammer Interstellar Hotel & Casino to receive two free Marsblood martinis (vodka, gin, triple sec, fresh raspberries and grenadine), with compliments from Mr. Hammer. Enjoy your visit!

BECOME A CREW MEMBER:

As a supporter of the museum, you will help to preserve MarsBlood in a secure and responsible manner. All humans, this generation and the next, deserve the privilege of seeing this strange, un-Earthly substance. Here at the museum, alien mystery is almost close enough to touch! Please stop at the Crew Member Kiosk for information on membership levels and benefits.

See Marilee Dahlman's story "Las Vegas Museum of Space Exploration" online at Metaphorosis.
If you liked it, leave a comment. Authors love that!
Remember to subscribe to our e-mail updates so you'll know when new stories are posted.

About the story

MarsBlood and mysterious cave art. If we ever discovered something beautiful, strange and incomprehensible on Mars, how would humanity respond? I decided to write something to answer that. The story takes the form of a museum brochure. So, step inside Las Vegas's finest museum seventy years from now and find out what we discovered on Mars, and what we did with it.

A question for the author

Q: What kind of pieces are the most fun to write (action, lyrical, etc.)?

A: If the piece is fun to write, hopefully it will be fun to read! I enjoy writing stories where 'stuff happens,' preferably action that's in some way funny or disturbing. I like flawed characters making poor life choices. Strange situations we've never actually experienced but can all relate to. Of course, stories where people wear dark capes or cloaks are always fun to write. When I hear 'lyrical,' I think poetry. I enjoy reading it, but haven't been brave enough to tackle writing poetry myself. Maybe someday when I've run out of ideas for stories about Mars.

About the author

Marilee grew up in the Midwest and studied English at the University of Minnesota. She spent ten years studying and practicing law in New York. She currently lives in Washington, DC, and when she's not working or writing, she's hiking, cooking soups from scratch, or seeing movies the old-fashioned way—in the theater.

The Girls Who Come Back Are Made of Metal and Glass

L'Erin Ogle

"Kate's back," says Lucy.

I look over and there Kate is, back from the dead yet again, even though there are rules about that sort of thing. No one else has ever come back more than twice. It's like three strikes and you're out—you've officially become too expensive or too troublesome to revive any more. But Kate's returned from dying at least half a dozen times.

"Again," says Lucy, rolling her eyes so hard her irises disappear. "For fuck's sake."

I don't say anything, but I squint so I can see Kate better. She looks like the same Kate, except more tired. She's hunching over a little more, but she's definitely here, even though we know she died two nights ago. Two nights ago, her body dangled limp from the noose she fashioned of her bedsheet, the other end looped around the railing she jumped from. Last month, she slit her elbows the long way on a screw she got ahold of, and before that she wrapped a plastic sheet (contraband acquired from somewhere) around her head.

"What makes *her* so special?" Lucy grumbles. She pushes her hair back, her own scars shining in a raised white slash across her neck. Lucy went straight for the jugular, she'll tell you, opened that baby up and died less than a minute later, even though people ran to press their hands to the twin jets of dark venous blood. But all that crimson just leaked between the spaces of their fingers. And Lucy died watching her blood creep into all the little cracks in their skin. It was the only time she tried to get out of here.

Dying hurts more the second time around, she says. They all say that. Not that much, I guess, since Kate keeps doing it. I wouldn't know. I don't remember dying. It must have been intense, because some of my bones weren't salvageable. The doctor repaired my skeleton with metal and replaced all my teeth with glass. They click together when I chew. I guess maybe I died on impact, smashed into smithereens. But I don't remember any pain, just floating through darkness, hearing waves breaking in the distance.

"How many times is this?" I ask.

Lucy shrugs. "Half a dozen? Maybe? Who cares?" After all, it's hardly interesting anymore.

I take a bite of dry chicken. The days here are long and they repeat themselves. We used to have better food, before Limited Funding. Now, lunch is always chicken or fish with aluminum-tasting vegetables for a side and fruit for dessert. Dinner will be a salad with fish or beef, cheap pudding to finish. Tomorrow, breakfast will be eggs and toast and fruit, always thick syrupy chunks of bland pineapple and peach poured from rows of cans stacked in the kitchen. There will be some kind of potato. There always is.

Monday is clinic. Blood draws and X-rays and sometimes we're inserted into machines to map our bodies. It's a long tube and the sound of its insides turning hums so loud it gets inside you and makes your whole body vibrate. Sometimes I can feel the metal inside me scraping inside my skin. Every day there will be Exercise, Group, Free Time. Friday is Movie Night. Everything repeating over, and over, and over again. Even the girls who die have to come back and keep living the exact same day, all those days stretching into the future and nothing will ever change. It's enough to keep some girls on the suicide train, but some of us don't want to die anymore.

There's a whole world out there, Lucy says in my ear late at night. We could go anywhere. We could do anything. We could be real, remake the world into a place for girls like us.

"Kate's back again," I tell Tamara. She's my counselor. I see her every Monday, Wednesday, and Friday after lunch.

"Is she?" Tamara says. She always answers my questions with another question.

"She is," I say. I pull my legs up underneath me and cross them. I touch the chair beneath me, soft against my fingers. I wish I could sleep here. My sheets are rough against my skin, like they're a clinic all their own, stealing skin cells and hair at every chance.

"How does that make you feel?"

"I want to know why she's brought back. Every time." I tell her.

"Does it bother you?"

"It just makes me wonder," I mutter.

Tamara doesn't answer, which means she won't say anything until I say something else. They say this is where we can say anything about anything, but there are rules here, just like there are rules everywhere else. You don't get to choose anything. You lost that when you offed yourself the first time and got brought back to participate in Research. There are lots of people who want their daughters to stop jumping off overpasses and swallowing handfuls of pills. Sort of makes me wonder whether I had parents that cared. But I don't remember anything at all before here.

"She's not even that pretty," I say.

"Is being pretty important to you?"

I shrug. I'm not pretty, but I'm not ugly either. I'm just here.

"I don't guess so," I say. "Not here, anyway."

"Why not here?"

I shrug. Because there are no boys here, except the doctor. But I don't say it. Lucy tells me to keep some things to myself. 'Don't let them see all of you,' she always says.

Every night, after the lights are out, we creep to the window. We look out through the bars at the fence, humming electrical wires topped with spiraling razor sharp wire. The girls who make it to the fence don't come back. Lucy says it's because the fence lights on fire and the bodies are burnt too badly. They bury them in a graveyard outside the fence somewhere, but sometimes I think I can hear them screaming. I'm not sure that's real. Sometimes I think it's just another sliver of me I lost on the return. Because when you die, you don't get to pick which parts you keep.

"The only way out is through the fence or the front door," Lucy says. Her eyes glitter in the moonlight. "But at the front door, they'll have people with guns. They'll catch us and bring us back. It's got to be the fence. Even if we don't make it, at least they won't bring us back here."

"No one's gotten past the fence," I say.

"We gotta figure out how to cut the power." When Lucy gets excited, static electricity forms in her hair and it starts to float all around her. "If we can get the power cut off, we could climb it. But we'd have to climb fast."

"How fast?"

"Fast as fuck," Lucy says. "We maybe would have two to three minutes after the power goes down. Because they'll have a back up generator. And the people with guns will come. Lots of them."

I press my fingers to the glass. It's cool and slick. I think about making it crack. Once, I broke a plate in half not even thinking about it. Lucy took both halves and smashed them to pieces against the floor before anyone saw. She says we can't let them see us, the things we've started to do. We came back with a humming blue ball of energy in our cores, spreading out along our bones and muscles and nerves. If they find out, they'll build bigger fences, build towers at each corner holding more men with guns.

I watch the fence for a long time, the trees behind it, the silver road winding through them, the big white sign that we can't see the front of, but then my own eyes start to blur and tear. I end up leaving Lucy at the window, her eyes fixed on whatever might be beyond here.

Next day, Kylie wakes us in the morning by shaking each of us gently. She's one of the nicer Carers; the others just holler at us to get up from the door. When I sit up, I see Kate, staring at the floor. She's standing next to Kylie, holding her sheets and blankets in a fat roll—I know inside of them are her sweats and shirts, two pairs of underwear, two pairs of socks. Her hair hangs in curtains on each side of her shuttered face. Kylie nudges her towards the single, unmade bed in the corner of the room.

"What the fuck?" Lucy says. Her eyes are red and tired. "What's going on?"

It's been just been me and Lucy for a very long time. Kate's always had her own room. Since the whole Limited Funding, no new girls have come. It might not have to do with the Funding. Maybe girls aren't killing themselves anymore, but I don't think that's it.

Kate doesn't say anything. Up close, she looks like a doll. Chalky white skin, eyes like blue shining marbles.

"Closing some of the wing!" Kylie chirps. "So, you get a new roommate."

"Fuck me," Lucy mutters.

"I don't want her in our room," Lucy whispers to me when we're showering. "She's going to ruin everything. They'll watch her all the time, which means they'll be watching us all the time."

But Lucy's wrong about that. It seems like there are fewer people to watch us now, and the ones who do are distracted, whispering to each other. Sometimes we overhear them whispering about Funding and Budget Cuts.

We're eating noodles and hard dry chunks of hamburger for dinner. They call it Stroganoff to make it sound fancy, but it's just chunks of beef and gluey noodles with some cream sauce. They like to name things, these people.

Like us. They call us the Stopgap Girls. We're sick and they are Repairing us. We are helping with Research, so girls like us don't cut their wrists or take Daddy's guns out of the safe. But now there are Unexpected Side Effects. There is no Clear Progress. No one wants to Fund us anymore.

"How come you've come back so many times?" I ask Kate.

Kate gives the slightest twitch of her shoulders. It's been four days since she moved into our room, and she hasn't said a word. She hasn't taken a shower, either. Her hair hangs slick with grease and when Kylie ran a comb through it this morning you could see each individual track the teeth passed through.

"Because she's not like us," Lucy says. She puts down her fork. Glares. Since

Kate came, I don't sleep in Lucy's bed anymore.

"What do you mean?"

Kate raises her head. She has gray eyes, the same color the sky turns outside before the rain comes. She stares at Lucy. Behind the glassy surface, something flickers in her eyes.

"I'm not sure," Lucy says. Her own eyes have narrowed to slits. Just the faintest gold brown iris rings her black, bottomless pupil. "But she's different."

Kate drops her head back down. I sort of want to scoot a little closer to her, show her we're not mean, but I also sort of want to be so mean she'll tell us why they keep making her come back.

"What happens if they close this place?" I ask Tamara.

"Where did you hear such a thing?" she asks, but her face is tight on her bones.

There is a mirror hanging behind her desk. It has a gold frame and there are people in it. They don't know about me and glass, that I am like glass, a shimmering sheet pulled over a shining structure. I can break and unmake things that are brittle. I can do a lot of things, but I'm not sure I'm supposed to yet. There is a reason for everything, I've decided. There has to be. Why else would I be here, playing a game where I only see half the board? That's why I listen and watch all the time. I have to know where all the other pieces are.

"I just wondered," I say. I can tell that what I've said has made her nervous, so I change the subject. "Why's Kate been brought back so many times?"

Something inside me, it's restless. Sometimes, I can hear an ocean in the back of my head. It whispers but I can never make out what words it actually says. I have to get up so I can blot it out, think for myself.

She dodges the question. "Do you know you're the only patient here who hasn't tried to commit suicide since you've gotten here? Doesn't that mean you're special?"

I am a model patient. (Prisoner.)

"Why am I here?" I ask her.

"You know why you're here. You tried to kill yourself, Tallulah. The doctor was able to revive you."

"But I died."

"Technically, yes."

"How long was I dead?"

"I'm not sure,' she says.

Minutes? Hours? Days? I can remember somewhere else, but not how long I was there. It was dark and powerful and it lives where there is no sun, just a big fat moon that paints everything the color of ash. There's a thing inside me that twists up sometimes, that feels dark and slick and mean, like shadows slipping over water.

"Tallulah," she says. "Without the doctor, you would still be dead. You would not be here, not any part of you. You're here to get better, so you can go home, so you can live again. You can see your family, your mother, your father, your sister."

'Do you remember anything from before?' They used to ask that, but they've stopped now. Because I don't. There's a ghost of a memory, of people maybe I used to know, but they wear no faces. I cannot think where I was before there was here. But sometimes I dream about a vast, dark ocean and a black sand beach. I wake up smelling something salty and reeking of rot.

Something inside me hitched a ride and now the metal and glass talk to me and turn to liquid at my touch, like the Doctor melted then into molds to make me new bones and teeth. But I don't need any help to do it. I think about that and I can see a small hairline crack in the mirror, up against the frame. I wonder if I put it there, and when?

Lucy and I go to the window again. The moon is full and the light of it makes the shadows of the fence thicker than usual. I can't see the electricity looping through its wires, a continuous circuit, like Lucy says it does. I can feel it all around us, though, flowing and pulsing like an ocean.

"Do you remember Before?" I ask them.

"No," Lucy says, so fast that it means she's lying.

"Tamara says I have a Before. That I have a family. But I don't remember a family. I only see shadow people and they don't have faces."

Lucy rolls her eyes. "We only remember what they let us." She shakes her head, her lies flat against her head. All day she thinks about the fence and getting over it, but she still doesn't know how. When I used to sleep in her bed, before Kate moved in, she even muttered about it in her sleep.

"Do you remember?" I call to Kate. "Before?"

She stares at me from her bed, her blue blanket against her face. Then she rolls over, but not before I see a tear glistening in her eye.

"Only three tubes today!" Kylie says, false cheer echoing in her voice.

The needle doesn't sting when she slides it in. It burns a little. I watch my blood shoot into the containers. It's vacuum sealed, which means they sucked all the air out of it so when my blood hits the hollow tube of the needle, it gets sucked in until the tube is full. Sometimes Lucy used to fight the Clinic and the tests, but she always lost in the end.

"Did you know I'm the only one here who hasn't tried to kill myself again?" I ask her.

She undoes the tourniquet around my arm with one quick pull. "Who told you that?" she asks, scooting her stool away, to face the ledge where she labels the tubes. Her tongue pokes out between her lips when she does that, pink against pink gloss.

"Tamara," I say. "She says that makes me special."

Kylie smiles. She's always smiling.

"Lots of things make you special," she says. She gives me a star shaped sugar cookie. "I saved you your favorite."

I bite into it, and I look at the tube where my red blood licks the sides of the glass. Being special doesn't mean anything, when I think about marble doll eyes, and the humming fence, and the sharp bladed wire on top. I think about oceans.

Kylie cries out. The tube she's holding has cracked, slivering into her finger.

The cookie melts sweeter than ever against my tongue.

Lucy is at the window.

I go to stand by her and press my hand to the glass. It feels the same as water in the tub, bending to the curvature of my palm. It fills the spaces between my fingers. I can understand it. Lucy looks sad.

"Look," I say, and I pull my hand away from the glass. It sticks to my fingers the way glue does, when I let it dry and pull it off in scabs.

She watches with her mouth open in a small O. Then she reaches out and touches a glistening piece of liquid glass. It retreats, snaps back into a hard shell. She looks at me. "Soon," she says. Her hair starts to hum again, flying up and separating into a halo.

If we leave, what happens to us out there? I don't sleep well. I keep hearing waves crash against the sides of my skull.

The Doctor is in Tamara's office.

"The Doctor thought he would join us," Tamara says. She forces a smile, but it stretches her face all wrong.

"Why?" I ask.

"How are you?" Tamara says, ignoring the question.

"Tired," I say. I can feel them studying me from the outside and something studying me from the Inside. I am not just a girl in an office. I am a girl or something like a girl in a cage, being dissected. They just haven't started cutting me open yet.

"Have you been sleeping well?"

"I want to go outside," I say to the Doctor.

"You go outside every day, don't you?" he says. He isn't smiling. He wears a mask of thoughtful concern.

"I want to go outside the fence," I tell both of them.

"Out of the question," he says.

"Why?"

"It just is," he says.

I think about shattering his face, but I settle for the mirror. It fractures into pieces and falls to the floor in jagged shards. Tamara shrieks and the Doctor steps in front of her. There's a sound, like a chair meeting the floor, behind the wall, a muffled scream. "I didn't mean to upset you," he says.

But I am upset. Upset travels through me, spinning out from millions of neurons.

"I want to go OUTSIDE!" I shout, and when the air bursts out of me it swells. The light bulbs rattle, then shatter, glass falling like rain. Shards fall on me and turn to warm liquid and I love it.

It's dark when I wake up. The moon has started cutting pieces off itself again, leaving a tiny crescent that sheds little light.

"They sedated you," Lucy says. She doesn't turn away from the window. "I told you, about showing them things."

The fence hums. It's loud in my ears. I get up from my bed, stagger a little bit. Whatever they gave me has left my head full and thick, cotton spread all over my brain. Frost has crept up the window pane, because we are in winter, cold and crisp, trapped in a glass snow globe that pulses with the beating of my heart.

"How did he seem? The doctor," Kate says.

Lucy snorts. It's something I picked up from her, how to make all your fury come out in a strangled sound. "That's what you finally speak about? The fucking doctor?"

"I know him," Kate says. "From Before."

Lucy's head whips around. "Liar," she hisses between her teeth.

Kate shrugs. Looks at me.

"Tell me about Before," I say without thinking.

"You know why this place exists, right?" Kate says.

We shake our heads, both of us.

"To fix this," she says, and taps her right temple. "The wrong part."

"What the fuck are you talking about?" Lucy says. She says *fuck* more these days, as if it might make her words heavier. More capable of inflicting damage.

"The Doctor had two daughters, once. He loved the first one the best. But she was Sick. She was always sad, or very angry. Then one day—" and here she makes a gun out of her thumb and first finger, angles it at the same temple she touched before, makes a sharp clicking noise with her tongue, "BANG." She mimes blood falling from her head, sticks her tongue out, her head slack on her shoulders.

"She died," Lucy says. "So, what? Everyone dies."

"He couldn't bring her back," Kate says. "So, he tried to forget her. They buried her under the dirt, and he decided he wouldn't let any more girls die. So, he made this place, where he could make them live instead. Fix them. But the girls kept dying. They always found a way. But when they came back, they could do things, like make things happen around them. Bend the air. Raise up water. Make electricity—" and she looks at Lucy, whose hair lifts just a little at the edges of her bob. "You could make it stop," she says, nodding at the fence.

"Liar," Lucy says, but it lacks conviction.

Kate's eyes are flat and glassy. Doll eyes.

"Shut up. Finish the story," Lucy says.

"I was an accident," Kate says. "He didn't want another little girl all broken like my sister. He and my mom were together, and then they weren't, and I didn't ever know him. But then I got sick. And when I died, he came and got me. And now I'm here, and I'll never be allowed to leave."

"The fucking doctor is your dad?" Lucyline's turned the same red as the cherries in fruit cocktail. Her hair stands straight up from her head.

Kate puts her finger to her lips. Her nails are ragged and torn at the tips. Bloody crusts crowd her cuticles.

All sorts of understandings happen fast, hung in the air like tinsel around a tree, same as the big evergreen they prop up in a stand every year when the snow falls thick and unfettered and we put things on it that we don't care about.

"He doesn't care about me," Kate says. "No one cares about us here." She turns her eye to the outside. "But they would. If...."

And she trails off.

"If what?" Lucy says.

"If we got out." Kate smiles for the first time I can remember, and it carves her face like a scythe ready to fall.

The doctor has placed a large piece of square glass against the wall. He wants me to break it.

I can see the hook of Kate's nose in him, but not much else. His eyes are liquid gray pools and I look to see if I can see his dead daughter lurking in the depths, but all I see is my reflection.

The glass does not crack. I don't want to crack it, and he wants me to, and he starts poking at me, trying to make the sore parts flare up into something bigger.

The doctor asks me about my mother. About my father. About the faceless figures that are my family, but the glass will not break. I harness the things inside me and pull back on the bits chomped between their teeth.

He thinks he's so smart.

If I die, I want veins sliced by translucent glass. I want to be cut open by sleek sharp blades. I picture a rough cotton sheet around my neck and shudder, I think of a rusty metal screw and turn brittle inside, ready to crack into thousands of pieces if it touches me.

"I have a plan," Lucy says, shifting her weight from foot to foot. Time is running out. We can all feel the walls growing closer together.

I'm looking at Kate, wondering how much of her is real and how much the doctor replaced. There was a movie once where this guy could change faces. He could be anyone, and he broke into places like this one. "Who are you, really?" I ask her.

Kate rolls an eye to me, one that has died too many times to feel much of anything anymore. "I'm just a girl that can know things," she says. "I can't do things like you and Lucy, but I can read people like books. Not even books. Maps."

"What fucking good is that?" Lucy mutters.

"Not much," Kate says. She turns her face away. "Your plan is for Tallulah to shatter the glass."

Lucy's gotten thin. She shakes under her skin all the time, even the moments we're alone and my fingers jitter across the sprung trap of her ribcage.

"We go through the broken doors and we run all the way to the rec room. We have to stop the fence. That's on you, Lucy. You're the one who can make your hair float. Then we throw sheets over the wires and climb."

"Why don't you talk to him? Your dad?" I ask her.

"Because I am alive and I shouldn't be," Kate says. "Because he won't let me die."

"I'll short out the fence," Lucy says, and her hair beams with electricity. The lights stutter twice in the hallway. "I can, I know it." Fire in her eyes. It sets something to burning inside me too.

I watch Kate. I can see her father in parts of her, and I don't know which part to believe in—the part of her that is a reflection of him or the part of her that hates him.

It's Kylie's last day. She won't tell us why, but Kate will.

"Funding Cuts again," Kate says, her smile carving up her face. "There isn't much time. Once the funding goes, they'll have to get rid of us."

When did she become our leader? There was nothing declaring that. It just happened, smooth as silk, very insidious.

"What's out there?" I ask Tamara, pacing.

"A world," she says. "One you wouldn't like all that much."

"How do you know?"

"I know," she says. But she's restless, shifty eyed, her muscles skittering under her skin.

"What happens when the funding runs out?"

Her eyes snap up. "Where did you hear that?"

Sometimes, it's better to just stop talking.

"Are you ready?" Kate asks us.

My skin prickles with life. I nod. I want to live out there, not end up a ghost in a graveyard

"Are you?" Kate asks Lucy.

Lucy peers at her from underneath her stood up hair. "Why are you doing this?" she asks. "He's your dad. How do we know you're not tricking us, that you're not with him?"

"Because he won't let me go. And I deserved better. We all did," Kate says. "We matter just as much as she did."

"Who?"

"Doesn't matter," Kate says, but I know she means her sister. The one he loved best. "It's time."

I close my eyes and draw everything inside me, like I am an ocean, preparing a tidal wave. Everything swells painful, power and energy huge and immense, inside my chest. When I exhale, all of it explodes from me. Sheet of glass shatter. Door windows blow out. Lights. Mirrors. The glass sings.

"Run!" Kate commands.

Lucy and I link hands, to sprint through the shattered door that separates our hallway from the main corridor.

Lucy holds my hand tight. We don't look back.

We run to the rec room. The huge window that eats up most of the paneled wood lining the rec room is already shattered, shards glittering on the ground. We climb over it and I hear Kate make a yipping noise, look back to see the side of her leg opened up in a gaping mouth. She clamps her hand to it, shaking her head. We can hear footsteps and shouting from the hallway.

Lucy puts her hand over the wound. Kate makes a hissing sound, and smoke trails up from where Lucy touches her. When Lucy pulls her hand back, it's sealed shut with a blackened crater.

"*Come on*" Lucy tells me. She lugs Kate to her feet, helps her shamble for the fence, and I follow them, my heart beating inside its metal cage.

We're at the fence. They're coming for us. I don't look back, but I see Kate clenching her teeth, looking over her shoulder. "You gotta hurry," she says. "You gotta do something. I forgot the sheets. We don't have enough time."

Lucy spreads her fingers out and energy flickers there in the space between them. She holds them palms up towards the fence, her face crinkled up.

Nothing happens. The energy doesn't travel to the fence. There's no surge. Even though her hair is sparking like crazy, she can't discharge it anywhere.

"I'm scared," she whispers. Her eyes are so beautiful.

I love her, I think.

"I'll try," I say, as they shout behind us.

"No time," she says. Her eyes fill with flames.

"Don't—" I shout, but it's too late.

She reaches out and wraps a hand around a line of fence. There's a hot tongue of fire that reaches out and slaps everything around us, but the big lightning crack arcs from the fence up Lucy's arm. She burst into flames, a burning torch capped by glossy black hair standing straight up.

She turns to me.

"Go be free," her charred voice sings in my head, and the fence dies in a shower of shedding sparks. The lines no longer hum and I place a foot on one, then my other foot on the wire above it. There's no time to be careful. I climb fast. I hear Lucy in my ear, telling me two minutes. Back up generator. Guns.

When I touch the curving barbed wire, it flattens for me the way glass does. I vault over it. Kate's only halfway up the fence. She's bitten into her lip, and blood runs freely down her chin. I wish it had been her that grabbed the fence. Not Lucy.

But Lucy would want me to help her. So I try to soften more of the fence at the top. It doesn't melt the way glass does. It bends but doesn't liquify. Then Kate's coming over the top. Her fingers slip on the wet metal. I grab her legs, making her scream, but she lets go, and we tumble to the ground.

She looks back at the institute. And she's shaking her head, tears running down her face.

"They're coming," she says.

Inside me, I can feel the wound splitting open, where I clung to Lucy and what would come after this. I can smell her scorched body, still smoking, but I don't look at it. I can't. I open my mouth to scream. I suck in air that seems to compress and just keep spilling into my mouth, until I am so full of it my skin feels like an overstretched balloon. Then I let my scream loose.

The air, patted down and packaged and forced to occupy a much smaller space, blows out and expands. It travels in a wave, and then they are falling down. Trees are falling down. The building shakes.

"Holy shit," Kate says. She turns her seafoam eyes to me. And she smiles, like she knows exactly what I'm thinking.

I didn't mean to do it. Did I kill them? But already, I can see the bodies stirring.

Kate's hand slips in mine. "I saw a place we can go," she whispers. "An old mill everyone drives by just down the road. It's full of things we can use."

Glass? I ask her, in my head.

"Glass, and metal, and lots more," she says. She grins again, and all that blackness that she brought back spins up inside her. "We can build our own world there. Or unmake it. Whatever you want."

It isn't what I want. It's what came back inside me. It hides behind my face and wraps itself around my parts. They are more metal and glass than muscle and bone. It wants things the way I want Lucy to come back. Fury digs a canyon in my heart, and I look back one last time. They are rising, their bodies loose limbed and stumbling, but they will come.

Lucy would want me to be ready.

We run.

See L'Erin Ogle's story "The Girls Who Come Back Are Made of Metal and Glass" online at Metaphorosis.
If you liked it, leave a comment. Authors love that!
Remember to subscribe to our e-mail updates so you'll know when new stories are posted.

About the story

"The Girls Who Come Back Are Made of Metal And Glass" was really predicated on one idea—a doctor raising girls from the dead who had committed suicide to atone for his own failure as a father. The characters took on a life of their own, and it became much darker than originally anticipated. If you were to raise the sentient dead, where had they been in between? What kind of place? And what else might have been there, waiting to come back as well?

It ended up being about the girls more than the doctor, about a yearning to be free instead of restrained, and about the insidiousness of evil, making a home inside of lives wrecked by good intentions.

As the girls came back, they left something behind that was vital, and brought back something sinister. Trauma creates cracks in the belief structure the world is a good place. If they're not healed, all kinds of things get in.

I was always rooting for the girls to gain freedom.

A question for the author

What is your favorite word?

There are so **many**. I'm a particular fan of 'lasterday' invented by my 5 year old instead of yesterday. Technically, she's right. But I love words that roll off the tongue, such as melancholy, soliloquy, lascivious, luscious, and my favorite 4 letter word, starts with F.

To pick one?

Doppelgänger.

About the author

L'Erin is a writer, mother, and ER/Trauma Nurse from Lawrence, Kansas. She has stories at *Metaphorosis*, *Syntax&Salt*, and forthcoming from *Pseudopod*, as well as various other publications. She's hard at work saving lives, working on a novel, writing more stories, and resisting the Trump administration and all that it stands for.

@Lerinjo

Copyright

Metaphorosis Publishing

Metaphorosis offers beautifully written science fiction and fantasy. Our projects include:

Metaphorosis Magazine

Metaphorosis, a weekly magazine of SFF short stories, including stories from all the authors in this anthology. Find out more at magazine.metaphorosis.com, and sign up to be notified of new stories.

Metaphorosis Books

Recent books from Metaphorosis can be found at <u>books.metaphorosis.com</u>, and include:

Score

an SFF symphony

What if stories were written like music? *Score* is an anthology of stories written to an emotional score.

Best Vegan SFF of 2018

The best vegan science fiction and fantasy stories of 2018!

Metaphorosis
2018

All the stories from *Metaphorosis* magazine's third year. Fifty-two great SFF stories.

Metaphorosis:
Best of 2018

The best science fiction and fantasy stories from *Metaphorosis* magazine's third year.

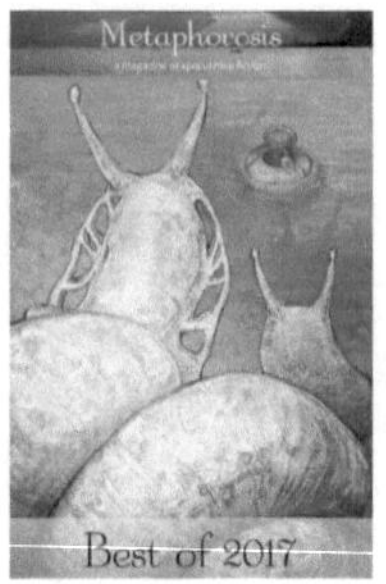

Metaphorosis
2017

Metaphorosis:
Best of 2017

All the stories from *Metaphorosis* magazine's second year. Fifty-three great SFF stories.

The best science fiction and fantasy stories from *Metaphorosis* magazine's *second* year.

Metaphorosis 2016

Almost all the stories from *Metaphorosis* magazine's first year.

Metaphorosis: Best of 2016

The best science fiction and fantasy stories from *Metaphorosis* magazine's first year.

Reading 5X5

Five stories, five times

Twenty-five SFF authors, five base stories, five versions of each – see how different writers take on the same material, with stories in contemporary and high fantasy, soft and hard SF, and a mysterious 'other' category.

Reading 5X5

Writers' Edition

All the stories from the regular, readers' edition, plus two extra stories, the story seed, and authors' notes on writing. Over 100 pages of additional material specifically aimed at writers.

Best Vegan SFF of 2017

The best vegan science fiction and fantasy stories of 2017!

Best Vegan SFF of 2016

The best vegan science fiction and fantasy stories of 2016!

Susurrus

A darkly romantic story of magic, love, and suffering.

www.ingramcontent.com/pod-product-compliance
Lightning Source LLC
Chambersburg PA
CBHW030208130726
47898CB00012B/937